THE World IS A High Hill

THE World IS A High Hill

Stories about Jamaican Women

Erna Brodber

IAN RANDLE PUBLISHERS
Kingston • *Miami*

First published in Jamaica, 2012 by
Ian Randle Publishers
11 Cunningham Avenue
Box 686
Kingston 6
www.ianrandlepublishers.com

National Library of Jamaica Cataloguing-In-Publication Data

Brodber, Erna
  The World is a High Hill : Stories about Jamaican Women / Erna
Brodber

    p. ; cm.
ISBN 978-976-637-564-5 (pbk)

1   Women – Jamaica   I. Title

305.4097292   - dc 22

Cover and book design by Ian Randle Publishers

Cover image *Goddess of the Crossroads,* oil on canvas courtesy of Clinton
Hutton. The symbol of womanhood is morphed into an all-seeing eye set in
concentric circles denoting the all-seeing godlike nature of the eye. The outer
circle indicates eternity (without end) and a method of knowing, being and
doing in opposition to the linear. These are set within a pyramid denoting
the hill of the world. It is surrounded by clouds and spiritual elements. The
symbol of the woman/goddess arms and body denotes the crossroads, the
realm for contemplation, for figuring out issues, for casting down troubles
and opening up new pathways.

Printed in the United States of America

Contents

Foreword / vii

Acknowledgements / xv

Beverley / 1

Cynthia / 16

Kishwana / 34

Lilieth / 61

Lily / 78

Mary / 93

Pauline / 103

Rosa / 116

Suzzette / 125

Ursie / 140

Vadney / 150

Valerie / 164

Interview with the Author
by Carolyn Cooper / 177

Foreword

I am thrilled to have been asked to write the Foreword to this latest literary production from Dr Erna Brodber – Jamaica's internationally acclaimed, multiple award-winning, cultural icon, social historian, novelist and sociologist. Her writings have both entertained and inspired, from 'Yards in the City of Kingston' (1975) and *Jane and Louisa Will Soon Come Home* (1980), through *Myal* (1988) and *Louisiana* (1994) to *Standing Tall: Affirmations of the Jamaican Male* (2003). *The World is a High Hill* continues to reflect her interest in community life (as for her, knowledge resides less in the individual and more within the community), gender, class and inter-ethnic relations in a former colonized (and now neo-colonial) space and to demonstrate the complexities in the everyday lives of less privileged Jamaicans constrained by, among other factors, geographical location, mis-education, racism, classism, sexism and 'politrix.'

As, like the author, I am a St Mary-born Arian, I have long understood the role of storytelling and oral history in the education of rural folks; the history and sociology lessons they provide; their recreational and entertainment value as well as their reflection of contemporary society. So I was eager to read these stories set, for the most part, in rural Jamaica; stories about, at one level ordinary, at another level extraordinary women who endure the twists and turns of life in Jamaica, but always with the ambition to better themselves, several doing so by moving to the city or abroad, at times in the not so motherly 'mother country' – despite being headed by a matronly Queen.

This Collection lived up to my expectations of a product of the pen of Nana Erna Brodber. Her fans will not be disappointed; and neither will new readers. The collection reflects Brodber's usual interest in the broader social world and in collecting and narrating folk stories. It testifies to her mastery over Jamaican languages, her familiarity with Jamaica's proverbs and folk expressions, linguistic creativity when confronted with phenomena that cannot be explained/expressed through the English language; with the role of colour in the 'two Jamaicas'; with the 'donmanship' phenomenon in our past and present politics; with the addictions in our society, including to church and marriage – no matter how long couples have been 'shacking up' or 'living in sin.' Some of the stories are set in the heady 1970s when all the talk was about 'power,' black or otherwise; and she invokes the philosophy and opinions of iconic figures – Paul Bogle, Marcus Garvey, Bob Marley, Walter Rodney, Haile Selassie I, among others.

The stories provide many teaching moments: moments in which readers will reflect on the author's boldness in touching taboo topics in Jamaican society like lesbianism; many moments that will bring laughter and many moments that will have readers nodding knowingly. An overview of the women's stories will illustrate:

I begin, as Brodber does, with Miss Kitty, who ensures that Mackie understands what 'making life together' really means. Miss Kitty is the mother of Beverley, who is ridiculed in Jamaica because of her very fair colour, but who finds acceptance first abroad and then, naturally, a 'yaad' after she 'stepped up inna life.' This turns the context of the bleaching culture on its head, but then, perhaps this is just an illustration that irony is part of Brodber's literary arsenal. Cynthia, armed with her UWI education and liberal ways, escapes with Machel to live where she believes, wrongly or rightly, that her inter-ethnic relationship will escape the scrutiny of her friends. Child of a don mixed up in '70s political culture, Kishwana's life demonstrates the complexities of existence in the inner city and the so-typical 'saving of inner city kids' represented by uptown connections/benevolence and education.

Lilieth is caught up in a love triangle and does not seem to know how to escape, although she knows why she should. Despite her university education and affiliation with the Church, she appears trapped by sweet mouth and apparently emotionally dependent Maurice Bailey, who, ironically, rescued her from his brother Freddie, her boss, but ends up getting her entangled in his emotional needs and married life; a web that neither Freddie nor UWI men appeared able to untangle.

Lily's story, like Lilieth's, will initially enrage true feminists; for she caters to Basil like a subordinate. But perhaps Brodber wants to reflect gender relations among some Rastafari. Lily's excuse is that, unlike her, he is a weak student who has to work and study with no time to devote to domestic chores. But he finds time for white Gerda, through whom he discovers (conveniently?) that there is not a black and white race, only the human race! He discontinues the admiration for his 'natural beauty' with her afro, and opts for straight hair Gerda. This meant no more Garveyism, dreadlocks, dashiki and Marleyism; no more Abena, only Lily; no more Basil Kwashee, just plain and more desirable to Gerda, Basil. The perennial, question is unstated but obvious: what's a girl to do when the big break-up takes place? Her life changes after Basil; however, for better or for worse, is for the readers to judge. The segments in this story that purport to give a glimpse into the social life at the University of the West Indies, where the author has spent some time – including goings on at the SCR – even if fictional, will cause the raising of that institution's collective eyebrows.

Mary chops the yard boy Andrew for being 'fresh' enough to want to do more than tend her garden and bringing her food when she is left alone by her husband, and, claiming self defence, lands in jail. Of course, if Mary had told the judge that 'Andrew was trying to get wife from her, he wouldn't have prisoned her, but she was too "hoity toity" to say things like that and believing some said, that she was Jesus own sister, she opened not her mouth and was sent to prison.'

Pauline's story reveals the pains of growing up and the almost inevitable, for some young girls, teenage pregnancy. Finding solace in the church, she leaves us in stitches as she describes the members and their class position or status, not to mention the behaviours that apparently go with them. Pauline does not remain a hopeless single mother, however, but qualifies herself to be independent and to become socially mobile. She was clear: 'migration must come'; [but] it had to be on her terms.

Domesticated and determined Rosa seeks out Zackie of Grenville town (which becomes Epsom for the convenience of the RGD) and takes up residence in his house because of a dream that she should. Patient and resourceful and intent on making life better for Zackie, she guides him to become more prosperous. Zackie's 'Saint Rosa,' is destined for heaven, if only for ensuring that, through surrogate Nita, his name would live on.

Suzzette gets pregnant at fifteen even though she is a bright and articulate teenager. She does not want the same fate to befall her own girls. She recounts her experience for posterity and perhaps for the satisfaction of her boss who is interested in such sociological issues and convinces her that she has an obligation to tell her story. This story brings attention to some Jamaican people's prejudices against people called 'Indians,' whether or not they are born in Jamaica; the inter-relationships between different ethnic groups where they live in the same community and the issue of sexual experimentation and even harassment that are features of Jamaican social life. Above all, it points to the reality of life in low-income communities – picked up again in earlier stories, about the reality of life where mothers and daughters are pregnant together and where large families live in cramped spaces with little privacy for adults and early sex education by observation for children. The ever-present village/urban yard gossip cannot be missed.

Ursie explains why she suffers from constant 'head shaking' – apart from the constant pressure from her aunt Jennie about her treatment of Carlton. Carlton has to finance the treatment of this condition medically and otherwise. The story reminds us of our cultural idiosyncrasies: taboo against sex; taboo about invasive medical examination; of hospitalization; What 'type' of women do men marry? Is a question that surfaces. Is it the ones who give them the time of day or the ones that do not?

Vadney's sister 'bucks' Vadney's husband and despite the hefty fine, feels justified, especially as he is both abusing

Vadney and trying to 'check her' while married to Vadney. Vadney after all is the pride of the family and the village, educated at Shortwood and holder of a salaried job. But her black passion without the black knowledge attracts her to a man she thinks can give her that knowledge because he parades it after returning from the USA – never mind that her sister thinks that 'knowledge and passion' are fake. Her husband is after her steady monthly cheque as it turns out and when that is not turned over to him, domestic abuse and the loss of the baby follow. Despite her sister's assistance Vadney stays with the abuser – a too familiar story – which gains the ire of said sister and wagging tongues of villagers. But Vadney was fortunate because other women had no 'bucker' in their family and would not walk out the back door or use migration as the route out.

Finally, we end with Valerie. Hers is a familiar story. A rural girl gets only so far in school and no further and is forced to seek domestic work to make ends meet. She gets work in the big house in the community where the big man has sex with her and she has a baby for him. But she leaves the baby with him and goes back to her granny. In this story, the big man without a name takes this baby to live with him in the USA she thinks. Valerie wants to borrow back the baby just to show her new man Harold that she could have a baby – for she needed just to prove who is the one that cause her not to breed after so long with Harold. A good Samaritan helps Valerie to 'migrate' – to make something of herself – but the search for the baby goes on.

The world is, indeed, a high hill – to climb – especially for 'low-budget people' in Buju Banton's creative formulation: black, rural, slavery-descended, miseducated, under-educated and downright uneducated, inner-city, downtown, working class people, men and women. Some of the women featured in these stories completed the steep incline, because they had no choice. They knew that for upward social mobility, '...migration should take place.' They also demonstrated by their lives that such migration '...had to be on [their] terms.' St Mary women (and not surprisingly Brodber's parish features in some of the stories), have long known this. Just as *Myal* is corrective, so are these stories, which provide an outlet for Brodber's teachings, her alternative knowledge system to the empowered bad words and ideas of those who would keep us mentally entrapped and devoid of black knowledge to nourish our black bodies threatened by what one critic described as 'cultural constipation,' the likely result of miseducation. Her corrective teaching is also done at her African-centred 'Blackspace' in Woodside, St Mary, a sanctuary and community intellectual space for all who are eager to learn at her feet and to reclaim or proclaim their voice and agency.

Verene A. Shepherd
Director
Institute for Gender & Development Studies
University of the West Indies

Acknowledgements

I wish to acknowledge and to give thanks for the help of Dr Laurence Brown of the School of History and Culture at Manchester University, England whose invitation to visit his programme gave me the time to compose these stories. To Bunny (Angela) Heron for reading this work and choosing its title. To Professors Verene Shepherd and Carolyn Cooper who have provided protection for this work fore and aft. To Clinton Hutton for so graciously selecting, photographing and transmitting to me one of his paintings which now graces the cover of this work. To Ian Randle Publishers for taking me in when I was adrift and floundering.

Beverley

$\mathscr{M}$iss Kitty was not someone you fooled with. She had come to Random from St Elizabeth with teacher and had struck up a relationship with Mackie. He had told her when Teacher was leaving for Salt Spring, not to go with him but to stay with him, Mackie, and let them make life together. With Teacher gone, it looked like Mackie had forgotten what he had said for she found herself in his house with their child and no ring and no date set to get one. Seems he didn't understand that 'making life together' meant a ring put on in church, and she had given him a good set of thumping and scratching and dragged him to parson. A wedding and three children later, Beverley had come, a pink baby with transparent skin, and hair like that between the corn cob and the corn trash. The people called her hair red but it was really more brownish yellow like a carrot. Miss Kitty was from down the country, from St Elizabeth. She was red-skinned like a lot of St Elizabeth people. All the other children had taken Mackie's hair colour and a black of skin which was a cross between her colour and Mackie's. Beverley had nothing at all for Mackie. And what she had didn't even look like it was from her. All she had for the family was the quality of hair – knotty.

The little baby was not odd to her, though; she had even seen straight hair, and hair the colour of ash that falls from the burning wood on human being's heads. She had also seen in her first child, hair like Beverley's but this had changed up with time to be black like that of the other children. Beverley's refused to change. There she was in the middle of seven children, for three followed her, looking and feeling the odd one out with her whitish skin and reddish hair. She suffered at home; she suffered at school and when Lord Kitchener's song about the redhead came in, big men were serenading her on the streets:

> Give me the redhead, redhead
> This is what I said,
> Give me the redhead.
> I must have a redhead before I dead

It really did worry her that big men might indeed be thinking of her little daughter in adult ways and Miss Kitty would have very much liked to fight them but she knew she couldn't go around thumping and scratching everybody. She just gave thanks that nobody had convinced Mackie that the child was not his and bring confusion into her household. They couldn't call any names for there were none but black-skinned people for miles around and for decades Miss Kitty had not left the area and had not gone home where there were red-skinned people. So there was no room even for speculation. What Miss Kitty did was to take her troubled daughter on her lap, rock her and tell her that God was not asleep; He had a good reason for making her what she was and she would soon find out what good thing He wanted her to do with her red hair.

The Big house was still the big house on the hill with the village houses around it though the people in them were now of the same colour. The Big house mistress knowing how well Miss Kitty had worked for teacher's family had asked if she would come and do their washing. She was not into that anymore; she had her own household to manage but Miss Kitty had personal knowledge of God's hand and saw this offer as a godsend to protect her daughter, and by agreement with the Mistress would send her on Saturdays to do some light work like dusting. No bother would trouble her there for the man hardly spoke to anybody: he would hardly see the child much less bother her and the little boy was at boarding school, too hoity toity to see her daughter much less touch her; she could rest assured for those hours. And the girl would be learning upper class ways that could put her in good stead one day.

When it came time for boys, none looked at her. Eyes passed over but none to stay and make four. She had very sympathetic girl friends but they were at a loss to know what to do with her. She couldn't take out her compact to refresh her face with powder for neither she nor her friends nor the store clerks knew the colour of the cake powder that she should buy. There was no point in her plucking her eyebrows for she could find no pencil the colour of her eyebrow with which to reshape it. It was the same thing with lipstick. There were all sorts of colours then, colours that no lips could naturally have, but they did go well with the dark of her friends' skin even tangerine, but nothing suited her. She had to resort to biting her lips to give them a bit of colour. Beverley was a misfit.

It was in England where she went to do a nursing course that Beverley began to feel less like a fish out of water. It was your accent that distinguished you from others. Beverley's was undoubtedly Jamaican, an identity firmly assured both from the perspective of her people and that of the English people. But one day and it happened on other days for she set out to test it, with her head tied in the way English women tied theirs and with her winter coat buttoned up to her chin and her mouth likewise, a white person did look her up and down and say: "Sorry, for staring. I thought you were my friend Victoria and couldn't figure out why she was snobbing me." Another time after she had said, she was not Victoria, the voice had commented, "If I didn't hear your accent I would say you were Victoria messing with my head." Since it happened when she walked on a certain road, she assumed that there was somebody living there that she resembled. This was a new experience: there was somebody who looked like her. The world was not such a lonely place any more for God had made more than one of her.

Like so many Jamaican nurses, Beverley migrated to Canada shortly after finishing nursing school in England. It was there that life began to turn around for her and she began to glimpse the special thing that her mother had said God had in store for her hair. Here she could find no West Indian hairdressers to straighten and curl her hair with a hot comb, as was the style among her peers. They were doing it themselves. Her own efforts had been disastrous and Beverley chanced going to a native, who straightened her hair chemically and styled it in the only way she knew how. In Canada as in England, the natives tried not to touch black people in the normal push and pull of travel lest the atrocious accent or the colour come off on them. On the subway with her now chemically straightened hair, Beverley felt a distinct change: she was being pushed rather than being skirted around; no hands off and separation from the foreigner as West Indians experienced! It seemed the Canadians saw her as one of theirs. It was a very simple event which grounded her in this feeling that she had at last found her colour group. Matron was talking in her hearing about the West Indian nurses. She wanted a meeting with them and had sent an aide to round them up. All her dark-skinned friends were referred to as West Indians but when they came to her name, Matron had said, "And bring Beverley Grey 'the redhead' who hangs out with them, too." She was not a Jamaican or West Indian as far as Matron was concerned; she was a redhead who only hung out with them.

After that she had overheard other persons talking about her and calling her 'the redhead'. Canada had the same name for her as her village people had, but it sounded and felt different here. Shortly after she learnt why – Canada had a space for redheads. There were television shows on beauty in which redheads were featured as a kind of beauty and tips given about how to be more beautiful as a redhead. She started reading magazines and finding there material on what colours redheads should wear; what make-up, lipstick, eye make-up, how they should treat their skin etc. She identified and bought and tried with positive effect. No longer the odd one, the ugly duckling, she was now the redhead one, the swan. She was now walking with her shoulders high. From the ease with which the Canadian doctors socialized with her compared to her more normal compatriots, she began to realize that she was more likely to be taken home to Mom by one of them than her West Indian friends. They were commenting on it too, sometimes in jest, sometimes in anger: "Now that you straighten out your hair and it can swing, them people here think you white." Beverley was now comfortable with herself but she wanted more from life.

The day when her mother, not given to tenderness, had been moved to take her in her arms, her father had stood near them and said, "Everybody want to be the 'est'; some want to be the prettiest, others the richest. You are the reddest." Her mother had cut her eyes at him but she knew that that comment was coming from the place of love. He had told his friends when she was going off to England to nursing school that she would come back a 'doctress'. That was impossible now but there was nothing to stop her from furthering her studies. She would leave Canada with a degree in nursing administration. There were not many people with such qualifications in Jamaica and her father could get a chance to say that his red daughter was one of the few nursing administrators in the island. She did quite well but didn't leave Canada nor did she try to get a job as a nursing administrator there. The task she gave herself now was to have the kind of fun which her ugly duckling self had denied her. She began with going to events organized by the Jamaican embassy.

There were concerts; there were lectures; there were receptions for visiting Jamaicans; there were social welfare projects to help to organize. Beverley became a trusted aide. One event put her on the lips of everybody as a good diplomat and a valuable part of the Jamaican community in Canada. At one function, luckily it was a small localized one, the high commissioner had had a little bit too much to drink and had become depressed and teary-eyed. She had been sitting close to him, had simply turned to him and said, "Mr High Commissioner, I think you need to dance," and had carted him off to the dance floor, then had signalled his driver to take him home, had gone with them and had prepared a potion that could make him sleep, had waited until he had fallen asleep before she left for her own home. Everyone had been grateful to her. She now not only went to events at the high commission but had tickets given to them handed over to her, so had gone to ballets, to conferences, to events put on by other embassies and her mind had been opened to world of intellectual inquiry. The high commissioner's wife who had not yet arrived to stay permanently, was happy to find when she visited, a diplomatic woman, and one with an inquiring mind to keep her husband company and a good nurse to boot. Beverley, she learnt, was willing to act from time to time as his hostess and even from time to time as his nursemaid, for the high commissioner was given to depression and tears would from time to time escape his eyes at the wrong time. High life had fallen into Beverley's lap and on occasion stayed there, teaching her how to express and enjoy her woman self. Her friends said she didn't need to work; she could let the high commissioner keep her, but this was not in her books: independence meant a lot to her and she knew that part of her attractiveness lay in her independence. Still, if the district could now see the redhead girl at whom they used to laugh! Photographs of her with this official and that went home so that her parents could see what the gift of red hair was doing for her.

And she had no intention of breaking up the high commissioner's marriage. What would she do with this guilt ridden man? One of his favourite guilts involved his wife. They had both been left and black in their youth. As a matter of fact it was this past that had made the present government select him for the post: he would be able to help the burgeoning black Jamaican population giving trouble in Canada and being given trouble, for his sympathies they thought were still left and Afrocentric. The high commissioner's trouble was that he no longer believed in leftist or racialized politics. He could tell nobody this, least of all his wife who in 'these days' still wore a big fat 'fro and African print. Mercifully she had given up the sandals. He would have to confess to her sometime. In the meantime he cried into his glass of drink and occasionally on Beverley's shoulder. Her time would come.

It came with the minister of tourism. He was from the prominent family which had lived not far from her in rural Jamaica but to whom of course she was invisible, just a little village girl who helped out now and again. He was the usual handsome khaki coloured chap who had gone to England to study law and had come back with a white wife whose externals had begun to embarrass him for it was black power days, and he had accordingly treated her so badly that she had gone back home. There was one child: a red knotty-headed girl with white transparent skin. She had taken her but he had gone back for his daughter, his only child whom he loved dearly. Of course he remembered the little redhead. She had sometimes been sent to help out at his house. He had been told not to touch her which to his pre-teen mind, meant 'don't play with her'. He had been very disappointed for he was the only child living at home. But there had been Winston. While this child came with shoes, Winston came with his ten toes, to rake the yard or as his parents liked to tell their friends, "to rake the yard with Derek for we don't want him to see manual labour as something others do for him." And they did touch and play, giving him a better feel for boarding school behaviour. Poor Winston was not important enough for him not to play with and here was this girl whom he was not to touch, standing before him. "Is this really you?" This was just the role model that his daughter needed. Beverley saw more than model. She saw 'woman' of the house which she had occasionally entered through the kitchen door. That would make her parents proud and that would serve the village a sauce. And she was going in on her own steam, with enough qualifications to allow her to walk out and into a great job if and when she chose.

She was going back to school. She had finished nursing administration; now she would do tourism management. Jamaica survived through its tourism product yet there were very few qualified managers. If after she married him, the minister lost his job by whatever means, she needn't go down with him for she would still have certificates and a means of making her living and still be attractive to him. When the high commissioner's wife came to stay, she announced that she couldn't find a more intelligent woman companion than Beverley and was full of praise for the help she had given her husband who knew he could depend on Beverley to be discrete. She really was diplomatic material! They both wanted to marry her off and felt that the minister could not do better.

Beverley honestly wanted to help Jamaica and really did feel that the tourism product needed to be enhanced. So did the Jamaican government, for they were busily setting up offices in all the significant capitals of the world – in London, in Berlin, in New York, Toronto. They would come for the tourists in their own homes and seduce them on to their national carrier and take them to Jamaica to spend. Nobody had to think too hard to find the body to head up the Toronto chapter. She had the technical training, she was a natural diplomat and she was a woman – what a good government they would seem, one which operated no glass ceiling – she was familiar with the Canadian culture and her appearance was non-threatening.

She could pass for Canadian as quickly as she could pass for Jamaican. Beverley was in. She was featured in the *Daily Gleaner* and her picture cut out and duly pasted into the scrapbook of prominent villagers that the village school kept. The School's Challenge Quiz for secondary school students run on the television, was soon asking who is the first and yet the only female head of an overseas division of the Tourist Board. Beverley knew she was capable but she also knew that her transparent skin and her red head had finally begun to work for her. God was showing his hand.

Her friends, the high commissioner and his wife, each for his own reason was still on to her about getting married to the minister. It was time for his daughter to start thinking about colleges and a career, so they invited her up to visit Canada to sample colleges. That would draw Beverley and the minister close, they thought. The daughter was really awful. She wore the most dreadful combination of colours, was dreading, not the kind assisted by hairdressers but that which you left to fall into any shape it wished and she would not wear a head scarf. She nearly made the high commissioner's wife, in the fear that their heads resembled, run off to get her hair straightened. The child did not need a role model, she needed a psychiatrist. With this thought Beverley realized that where she had handled her ugly ducklingness by shrinking away, this child was trying to deal with hers by putting it in everybody's face. She would work with that.

Cathy would be a model, a face of Jamaica. A kind of pre-Rasta model. Around her there would be a seminar about the Rastas in Jamaica; there would be Rastafarian music and food and of course what everybody wanted to know – a lecture on the Rastafarian woman. Was she subjugated as so many studies said? The social studies departments of the universities, the fledging Rastafarian community in Toronto and even the middle class Jamaican Canadians who normally wanted to run away from Rastas, would come out to these lectures, if only to dispute the significance of Rastas in the culture. Cathy was no Rasta but she had so often been taken for one, that she was willing to parade herself at conference, social get-together, whatever the office planned, as one. The girl had a voice. Untrained, but the potential was clear. Like every outrageous youth she was a songwriter, had tapes and CDs and was waiting to 'buss'. Beverley chose to take her art seriously and got a West Indian musician from York University to sit with her and if possible turn one of her pieces into something that could be performed at one of the Tourist Board events. He thought she had some talent and managed something to Cathy's delight. There was a band behind her; she was announced as an up and coming singer and songwriter. Nobody quite knows what the standards in music are these days, so Cathy's odd off-key notes were well received as perhaps the new 'genre'. The minister was there. He wouldn't swear that his daughter could sing but he was sure that she was happy for one of the only times. And this was due to Beverley. He would be forever in her debt.

Beverley thought it was time for her to find out whether it was only 'in her debt' that he wanted to be, and would now give small private parties even the occasional two person dinner, to check the standing. Nothing happened despite the assistance of the high commissioner and his wife. It was the awful redhead, now almost happy, that gave her food for thought. She in her undiplomatic way told Beverley that she knew that there was a plan. One part of it had worked and she was grateful, for Coleman was taking her on and would take her as far as she could go with her music. "If you hadn't decided to try to please my father by taking me on, I would not have met him. I have doubts about your ultimate goal though. It was not just white women that my father tired of, it was, I think, women. This is my opinion and that of my mother. You don't have to take it. I must warn you though that I like, no, love my father and that I don't think he wants to be what he probably is. He's been on the psychiatrist's couch. Because of him I started reading about these problems and I think he is on something that suppresses his sex drive. Should you or any other woman disturb his equilibrium, he would be in social and psychological distress and I would get very negative towards that woman who created a need that he couldn't fill through her and have him searching in anti-social waters for satisfaction." Beverley knew this awful redheaded girl – weren't redheads supposed to be passionate – could get passionate indeed and she did not want to be near that passion. The private parties ended.

It was the minister himself who invited her to the next private dinner. He noticed that she had stopped inviting him to her place. Had his daughter been speaking to her? Speak the truth and speak it ever cost it what it will, she had learnt, so she told him the truth. When in the course of the evening he handed her his wallet, she thought she was now being given a new task – to extract the minister's credit card from his wallet and pay the bill. "Go to the photographs" he said. She looked. He handed her his blackberry and said the same thing. She looked. In each place there were stacks of pictures of fine looking adolescent boys.

"I know you had found me attractive as a man and had

even entertained, supported by my friends, ideas about marriage. Can you still like me?" he had asked. And she had no difficulty in telling him "yes" but she didn't think she would contemplate marriage any more. She could be a very good friend as she already was.

Their dates continued; she played hostess to him on his trips to Canada and even went home and did the same. Their names were twinned and the rumors started. There were even newspaper articles telling the date of the wedding. Her father remembered his conversation with her about being the 'est' and said that he hadn't mentioned the 'highest'. She was now that – the highest woman in Jamaica. A woman should not be as high as her husband. He hoped that she was only the 'highest woman' and that there were high men around for her. "Yes. There is, but the situation is hopeless," she would have told him if they could discuss such things together. She continued to be hostess and friend to the minister of tourism even after he became the shadow minister but an Italian ambassador coming to Jamaica without a wife and being very interested in the society, asked her help in getting to know the country. She was not in the diplomatic service, only still at the Tourist Board, and with the change of government had been brought home to the home desk. Nobody could stop her from showing a possible source of tourists around the island.

She and the Italian sometimes tested double rooms, had breakfast and dinner together in these double rooms and as they got to know each other better and he to know at least one member of the Jamaican society well, the insides of several hotels. They graduated into testing double beds and even single bed a la Bob Marley's song. He invited her home to Italy to test that country's offerings of hotels rooms and beds though they both knew that Jamaicans were not going to leave Jamaica in any numbers to be tourists in Italy. It was there that he got his marriage annulled for he had married a non-Roman Catholic; there that she took his religion and they got married before he came back to his posting in Jamaica. A Jamaican with her skills was just what the Italian embassy needed. Her father didn't think she could get any higher, for she was now not just the highest Jamaican woman but the very highest woman. They took to buying the *Jamaica Observer* for she was so often on page two. She was called the 'svelte redhaired wife of the Italian ambassador'. Nobody even bothered to mention that she was Jamaican.

Her parents knew who the 'svelte redhaired wife of the Italian ambassador' was and this was not a selfish family – the village knew too for Beverley never thought it hard to visit them in her foreign-made car stepping out with her careful linen suit, her arms full of gift-wrapped packages for the church's charity drive. The family managed to conduct quite a bit of their business at the gate, an Italian word falling accidentally from Beverley's lips now and again. "Ciao" in fortissimo became goodbye as if she was saying goodbye to the whole village. Go to Random today and people are still saying "Ciao" to each other when they mean 'goodbye', giving trouble to the PhD student in linguistics who is today about to write about the Italian occupation of Random without knowing that a little redhead girl single-handedly put that word in the village lexicon.

Then there was the evening etched in the memory of Random, when the long black car with the yellow licence plates stopped at Lester High School, about two miles from Random, and the uniformed chauffeur opened the back door and handed the lady passenger to the welcoming committee comprised of the headmaster, the chairman of the school board, the members of parliament for the area, the mayor and the custos, for Beverley had accepted the invitation to hand out the presents at the school's award ceremony. She gave with the left and shook with the right without a mistake. Nor did she forget to kiss the little brown-skinned girl with the drop-curled hair who handed her the basket of flowers. When Beverley flashed her red straightened hair out of her eyes to do the kissing, Miss Kitty squeezed her husband's hand and thought that her transparent skinned, red knotty-headed daughter would not have been asked to hand out a basket of flowers but here she was being presented with the basket of flowers. Then she thought she knew her husband must be thinking "How high can you get!" Then she thought another thought, "Pity the husband could not be here for all to see what the transparent skin and red knotty hair had brought her" but she squeezed it back into her head for God did not like greedy and look what he had spared her to see: Custos's granddaughter curtseying to her red knotty-headed daughter whom everyone had laughed at or at best pitied, with the whole of Random and the adjoining districts looking on, for Lester High School was the one secondary school around, serving villages as many as ten miles away, and the awards ceremony was an event which parents and friends did come to in truck loads. Miss Kitty was pleased with God for He had repaid her trust in Him without her having to thump and scratch anyone.

Cynthia

I was no Sophia Loren, not 36 by 21 by 36, but I did get my whistles on the road from the men around. They hailed me as "Slim" referring to my body and sometimes they did give me compliments on my hair which was thick and when straightened, could fall over my face and touch the nape of my neck. I knew how to sew and to make my 34 by 21 by 34 look good. People liked to say that women dressed for men but with this girl child it wasn't so; I dressed for myself and I didn't get caught up in "he likes me in heels, so I wear heels." I wore heels a lot as it happened but it had nothing to do with a 'he'. My feet didn't like flats perhaps because something was wrong with the arch of my feet. In any case, I loved leather – belts and shoes and the most stunning patterns came in heels. So I loved and bought heels whenever I could.

I had heard through my female friends that the men talked about my well shaped bosom. They reported an incident to me: I was athletic, holding the record in the university for the marathon for two years so far, and for that you trained hard. This guy was looking for a running partner and they suggested me. When he finally found out my identity, his answer my friends grandly told me, was that instead of running with me, he would have to run behind me so he could watch my bum and since he wouldn't be able to keep his eyes from it, would be on the ground within minutes. I wouldn't do. My bum like my bosom was attractive to men. I heard nothing of this kind from the mouths of the fellows I talked to on campus. Instead what I heard was, after I had read my paper to the class, "Cynthia where did you find that material?" Or while one was preparing his paper, "Cynthia can you point me towards some material on…." I was officially in political science, a course full of men and I never once felt any one looking at my body. I was one of them by brain, and that my own experience told me was the key to my happy relationship with my male colleagues. I loved my colleagues and I loved my programme and read just about anything that had to do with it and more, and I was getting quite a reputation for my knowledge of far eastern affairs. A first class degree and postgraduate work were inevitable. I was already putting out feelers and had hopes of going to where Arthur Lewis had started his career and Edwin Lewis and Vaughan Jones, my lecturers had been students.

I had as much rhythm as anybody who looked like me and I did dance and professionally too, so getting asked to dance at a party was never any problem, but this party dancing looked to me more sexual than artistic and I couldn't see why some person whom I did not know, should be so close to me that he was breathing in my ear. But I did enjoy parties. I liked the conversation and I liked party foods and the books in the house where the party was kept, so that while my girlfriends arranged themselves on the chairs so that their best side could show or tried to send vibrations or to receive them from the males, I was more likely to be curled up in a corner reading the most recent copy of the *Economist* that I had either taken with me to the party or found in the host's library.

My friends – let that be girlfriends – said I was strange:

"You've got the best body on this campus, but you have refused to use it." I didn't quite get what I was to use it for. Life was good. I was always winning on the track and in my classes. Was pushing myself further and further and getting into more joy. I was not the greatest dancer but I was good enough to be a permanent part of the troupe. I loved music and could afford to buy the CDs I wanted to hear, and had a good enough set. What more did I want? To learn to play the tuba. The school had just got a visiting professor whose special area was the tuba. I joined his class and my friends said, "What's with you? Why couldn't a guitar or a violin do for you. The tuba, yuck." Then they wondered, "Could it be the tuba teacher." This is where catty Catherine came in with her philosophical musing, "Any black man or woman our age who can't find mate, is waiting for someone outside of the race." "That's not me," I thought as I remembered my Chinese friend and her struggle to marry the black man she loved; how my father had helped to hide them from her parents and how he had said to me after all the hulabaloo, "I hope you know that if you did what your friend has done, I would be reacting just as her parents are reacting." No. This would not be me. I was forewarned and in any case, I was not waiting for a man of any kind.

I had not dated on campus, did not have that thing called a boyfriend but now I was going out with Machel, the tuba player. Actually, I did not see this as dating. It wasn't like what my girlfriends talked about – the romance, the special dress, the great place that we are going, the fantastic place which cost so much for a glass of orange juice and how he must love me if he is willing to spend so much on me. Machel and I just went to performances and

I went in anything that I would wear to lectures, even what I had just worn to the day's lectures. More likely than not, Machel was not paying for me. The tickets we used to go to these concerts were complimentary tickets given to him or to the school and nobody else wanted to go but me. And if he was going, why not go together?

Don't get me wrong, I like going to the fantastic places but it was more the challenge of going where improverished black students were not expected than a date where someone paid his week's food money to be with me. When my friends were twisting their lips around French words to place their orders in the swanky hotels that we loved to invade, I would embarrass them by asking for ackee and salt fish and I would never know what wine goes with what kind of food for I didn't like wine and to the surprise of most of them, my shocking order for mint tea or hot water with a bit of lemon, was usually easily served. I loved shocking and embarrassing my friends but I did actually like Jamaican food and things. Machel, the visiting professor, liked or wanted to like these things and was always willing to go out to find curried goat. He had a car and wanted to go out; I had no car and wanted to go out to the things we both wanted to do. We were prefect companions.

The chorus was on to me: "So is true, you really was waiting for white man! Chile you nuh know sey all of them people de bent? Whe you ah do wid him. What him a go tek breed you, mi dear? Him nose? Moreover dem man de mean. Dem even expect you fi pay for yu food when you go out with them and pay half of the taxi fare." Even the man-in-the-street was on my case. Walking towards Emancipation Park with Machel one evening, an elderly man looking like he could be a member of my family, said to me, "We never send you to school fi you go dash wey yourself pon limey sailor, you know." Thinking I knew him and he me, I was trying to place him, until a woman crossed the street and entered the conversational space and contributed, "Albert, lef de people dem alone. You nuh know dem from Adam. Who appoint you fi say who can love who?" Then she turned to me and patting me on the shoulder said, "Ah jealous, dem jealous. The whole ah dem wish dem coulda get white man or white woman. See Albert deh. Come back from England and vex sey no white woman never want him and him have to come back without one. No pay dem no mind."

When they had left and we felt we could step off, I said spontaneously to myself more than to my companion, "Jamaica does not like mixed couples." To which Machel responded as if I had been talking to him, "That's not what the data show. Notice that only one said uncomplimentary things. The data say that fifty per cent of Jamaicans don't like mixed couples but the rest allow that any people can mix as long as it is love." That was Machel: he could turn anything into a positive and a chuckle with it. Of course my friends were never told about such events, much as I found these little plays amusing and would have loved to share them. I missed my friends. We had come in as freshmen and been in the same rooms on the same block for two years. I didn't think Machel could appreciate these situations in all their fullness, the occasion for instance when looking vegetables in Papine market, a big tall very dreaded man seeing me with Machel, hailed me like the angel to Mary saying "What is the daughter of Israel doing with Shechem, the Hivite?" I prayed that Machel was not a

Bible reader and did not know what punishment Israel had meted out to Shechem for messing with their sister. They would have loved the scene where Machel stopped the car, came out and walked back to the corner to tell some young men who had been hurling racial abuses at him, "I am not a limey; nor am I a yankee, I'm a frog. That's the bad word for people like me who come from France." Then he tried to give them a geography lesson on France. My friends would have cracked their sides as I recalled such occasions for them.

Whether Machel was tired of these interactions or whether he thought our relationship was ready to go a notch higher, I do not know, but we now took less walks on the road and were now attending socials at the home of his friends. He must know, I thought, every white man in Jamaica, certainly in Kingston, who has a black wife or steady companion. Every Friday night it was somebody else's house and they were all there. Can't say I too much liked them but there was always something new to learn and I am into learning. The women sat apart from the men, so segregated you'd think they were Muslims. You could distinguish the man of the house from the other men: he is the one wearing the apron, the kind which you tie at the back of your neck and around your waist. Why did he need an apron to serve drinks or did he do the cooking too?

It was a variegated set of whites. And of course accents. They were from several parts of the United States, from parts of Europe, from Great Britain and from Australia. I learnt that they prized distinctions between them that I had not heard of in all my reading of their novels and their history. There was a conversation for instance in which there was a mention of 'the continent'. Something happened when somebody was on holidays on 'the continent'. One American voice apparently saw red, for he was asking quite loudly, "Where the hell is the 'continent'. Was this North America, South America or Africa?" Didn't they recognize that something happened in 1776, he was asking on the top of his voice. There was much apologizing and much hushing. In the woman's group, someone asked, "So what's so hot about 1776?" The voice belonged to Jade, his girlfriend, skin black as coal, hair like a cat's and a figure beauty queens would die for, tonight enhanced by a very black, very tight all-in-one. He was always talking about 1776, she shared. Would someone enlighten her, she asked for she couldn't get him to talk about it. Nobody did.

The women amazed me. They talked all the time about their men. These men didn't seem to have names. They proffered general statements about them. It was 'white men' don't understand this or that; 'white men' don't eat this or that; you can't expect them to know this or that for they are 'white men'. They knew the behaviour of men of other colours too for someone may talk about what a man had done and you might hear with a shake of the head, "He isn't white? A white man would never do that" or "Got to be a black man. Only they would do that." They didn't seem to see their men as people. I had often heard that white men who married black women saw them as trophies. But here I was seeing something else: white men as trophies, apparently chosen for their skin colour. I had to confront one who felt she had advice to give me as a neophyte. She was advising me to hold on tight to Machel for there were Jamaican women out there who were just dying for a white man and would take mine away at the drop of a hat. I did feel as if I was betraying Machel but I had to tell her that the black women I know, and I knew many of them, thought of white men as effeminate, homosexuals and tight fisted. I couldn't see anyone wanting to steal one. All went quiet and Helen who had forced this statement out of me, closed the conversation off with, "We know different types of people" and me responding with, "Apparently."

Machel had noted the contretemps between us and on our way home had shared that Helen and I did really know different types of people for Earl, Helen's husband had found her in a house of pleasure. "Cynthia," he had continued, "I know we white men are not much but we do seem to some people to have money. Surely you can imagine that a white man would seem a good catch among Helen's friends and worthy of being stolen away. In a sense then, Helen is right and I am happy to know that I am stealable." I noticed too that some among the men looked uncomfortable and learnt that the Irish are still seen and see themselves as inferior to the rest of the British. Machel informed me that not so long ago there were signs in Britain saying dogs and Irish not welcome. "How do you know who is English?" I asked him. I was to learn that they could look at the length of each others arms and legs, the colour of the hair etc. and say who was whom. It was totally new to me and I wondered who would tell those black wives talking about 'white men' this and 'white men' that, that white men did observe distinctions between each other. What 'white men' seemed to share totally was their love of beer. Good for Red Stripe and the local economy.

We no longer spent so much of our Friday evenings with the mixed marriages. The university had housed Machel in a two bedroomed flat. The extra bedroom became mine on Friday evenings. My friends were scraping their throats as if to say "Things are developing sexually" but they were not. We were two small children let loose on the world. If I wanted to get up at 2 a.m. and go running, Machel's shoes were ready. If I thought the air would be lovely at Catherine's Peak, we took a loaf of bread and some fruit and drove in his battered volkswagon up to Catherine's Peak to catch the morning sun and have breakfast. We might even take the tuba and charm. The tuba was happy, for it didn't get much of a chance to feel alive outside of the classroom and the occasional concert. We couldn't expect the neighbours where we lived to like the tuba. The birds didn't mind. Nor did the fish, so we were the first ones on a Saturday morning at Hellshire Beach. We played to the fish and the dread fishermen who gathered round us. I was surprised that no one seemed to mind that we were of different colours. Machel had an amusing and pithy conclusion: "Jamaican dreads love music more than they hate white men or seeing white men with their daughters."

Machel liked to swim, to snorkel and could not understand how a person like me could live on an island and not be involved with these arts. I am a learner and was ready to learn. Once more we were linked with the mixed marriages. Not the black part but the white. The wives came to the beach, but to pose, for they couldn't let the water touch their hair and couldn't swim well enough to keep their heads above the water. They were also there to get the midday meal – fish, bammie and coconut water. It was I and the 'white men' who did the swimming and the snorkeling. It was out of all of this experience that my hairdresser stopped getting my money. What a horrible smell when the sea water hit my straightened hair! It was my hair that was giving off that smell. I know, for I carried it around with me and could smell it when I was by myself under the shower. I could blame it on nobody else. It was my hair smelling like that. I started washing and shampooing my hair myself. This became part of Friday night. I can imagine what catty Miss Catherine would have said if I had told them that it was with the washing and shampooing that Machel and I inched closer to adulthood. It was now left for them to wonder what my knotty head in the open campus meant. "She couldn't be going rasta and still walking with the white man. And we know that it isn't Pentecostal for that and the Friday night thing simply can't go together."

Machel was fascinated by my hair. When black hair is very clean and submerged in water, it makes a noise like a curtain rustling. Certainly mine does. Machel would put his fingers in my hair and massage the scalp so he could better hear the sound of my hair. Then he wanted to be submerged in it. He put his nose into my hair and exclaimed at first and every Friday night after, that it smelt so good while I was saying to myself as in the old commercials, "Thanks to Breck." Now, nobody, not even my own mother had ever told me that my hair smelt good. Notice that he didn't say "It smells better than before." This guy was like that, embracing the positive and forgetting the negative. Machel wanted total participation in my hair. He would part this thick mop into small sections and dry my scalp with a towel and then the fun part for him: combing it out with my pick. I enjoyed that to no end and made it into play acting. He was my mother attending to my hair. I showed him how a Jamaican mother did the hair fixing ritual. I would open his legs and sit on a low stool with my head in his lap and his legs hugging my shoulders. He had more protrusions than a nose.

My tuba lesson had begun in October. I didn't go home in December of that year. I went home at Easter. My father was his usually dour self but so was my mother too and that surprised me. They are unequally yoked and not very happy together. Perhaps not happy apart either and they have such different personalities. As I get the story, Dadda was a thriving tailor. When ole Master Cameron was around, he was his tailor and tailor to the son, Master Owen too and even tailor to Mrs Cameron and Miss Althea, the daughter, for they were wearers of coat suits. Friends of their family would patronize Dadda as well and he became a kind of find for them – 'that treasure secreted in the deep rural area that only certain people can have access to'. Then as is the way of all flesh in Jamaica, when Mr Cameron died, Althea came and took her mother to the city or to England or somewhere but it was out of our village and away from patronage of my father. The outcome was that Dadda's business went downhill. Locals, even if they recognized Dadda's genius in cutting and sewing, couldn't or wouldn't pay him. Most didn't want well tailored clothes any how; they preferred to buy the cheap things in the stores. Dad went off to England to try his hand there but since Mama wouldn't come up, he came back down to the downsized business.

Mama on the other hand was flowering. He had picked her up, a fairly young thing, seen that she took her third year exams and through his relationship with Mr Cameron, got her a little teaching job. In time he got her to go to Mico. She was giddy-headed but she scraped through her exams and was able to get another and better teaching job. People liked my mother, she was indeed charming and easy to get along with, so she was able to move from elementary school teaching fairly quickly to high school teaching in one of the many secondary schools the government had just built. By this time she had a monthly salary that looked quite hefty and Dadda virtually had nothing. So there was this young giddy attractive teacher climbing the social and economic ladder and poor Dadda, considerably older than she was, walking behind her. Mama even stopped going to the one place that Dadda knew himself to be wanted: church. Dadda was a deacon in the church. Mama stopped going to church as she progressed; she needed her Saturdays for other things. Many meetings were indeed called in her job for Saturdays. I knew Dadda to be odd, sticking to an old-fashioned Garveyism; he had been unhappy in England and never pardoned white people for this, though Master Cameron had been white and had been helpful to him. In any case he had long given me his speech on racial mixing. I would have expected him to have the official talk with me, not my mother who by now was an expert in the Ministry of Education on social studies and meeting Canadians and Americans on a regular basis as they funded this and that part of her programme. Nevertheless, it was she who called me. Said she wanted to talk.

"I called you some weeks ago. Was a Friday night I think. The porter couldn't find you for a long time and then I asked for Valerie for I knew she would know where you were. She gave me a telephone number and told me that on Friday nights you are likely to be here. I called the number but got a foreign male voice identifying itself with a strange name. I tried several times and got the same voice and name asking me to leave a message. I knew then that I had the right number but I didn't leave a message for I couldn't understand why you would be at a place for the night with some white man." My mother is not a patois speaker except when she needs to be very expressive. She obviously needed to be now.

"So you de wid white man?" That was what she wanted to say. And she was lying. There is just one voice that IDs phones in Jamaica. And it is not a male voice. Moreover I knew from telephoning it often, that Machel did not even have an identifier on his phone. Mama was protecting someone. I supposed that Valerie had informed her of my relationship with Machel and she wanted to discuss it without giving Valerie away. I got very technical with her.

"'De wid' as you know Mama means sharing your body with a male person and he sharing his money with you. I am not sharing my body with any one and no one is supporting me financially besides my scholarship money and what you occasionally send for me." She was not content with that, so I told her what I could about Machel. She was glad, for now she could get on with her business, and her business was to hand me a lecture on black/white relations in Jamaica such as she couldn't hand her student teachers nor those with whom she sat to write textbooks. Her greatest anger was the lies told on black men, that they were the uncaring cause of the mother-headed, single woman family. "White men are the creators of that and they have the temerity to write in their books that the black family is weak, for black men do not support their children and their mothers, and are shy of the kind of commitment that married people make to each other. All them black people name Neuville and Champaigne, where them get those names from? Is people like your friend that come here, use the woman dem, breed them and then gone back to France or wherever. Sometimes is the black man self who have to father these white men children. And still they get bad name."

I had not been told until then the true history of my family. "You know what you great-grand and your grandmother suffer? Your great-grandmother had to go wash for this old beat up backra and she had to do more than that. Of course she get pregnant for the man, for though he is a big man he never bother to use any form of birth control, for is a black woman and she don't count and his nastiness can get into her womb or wherever he feel like putting it. Your great-grand wasn't even fifteen good when that dog make her into a mother. Your grandmother was bright and win a half scholarship to high school when she was twelve. Your great-grand go to him for help to find the other half so she could go to high school. The man run her. Big property owner! 'What the wench want with school? You want to give her high fallutin notions about herself? There is plenty of work she could do here. She have no need fi go get training fi do any else work.' Your great-grandmother never even make her take any work on her father plantation for she didn't trust the man not to rape his daughter. Is them kind of people you dealing with." What else could I say to this ancestrally angry woman but "Thanks." She didn't seem to require more. We were very pensive for the rest of the vacation but there was no more question about Machel. Towards the end, we were our old selves again, she beating me at checkers and me her at whist and my father winning at Scrabble.

Nothing changed with my white man and I. I told myself that his contract was nearing the end and whatever discomfort our time together brought to other people, would soon vanish. It wasn't as easy as that and Machel gave voice to this thought. "My leaving won't settle any issue. I have never had a relationship as pleasant and stress free as I have had with you and I daresay you have never had one so pleasant and stress free as you have had with me. It will be difficult for you to give me up and difficult for me to give you up." He had got me to talk about my mother's lecture. He added now, "I know we are not engaged or anything but I did write and tell my parents that there was this girl…You will be pleased to hear that my mother holds a view about us parallel to that of your mother: 'These entrapping black women. I should have known what would happen to you.' They are both against race mixing but where your mother sees your 15-year-old great-grandmother as a victim, my mother sees an oversexed teenager who insinuated herself into the kind master's bed and there single-handedly impregnates herself and blames it on the master."

"The world is a high hill and we are sitting on it all by ourselves," I said aloud to myself.

Machel responded, aloud to himself, "I do like the air."

We agreed that we wanted to continue to be in each other's lives and that we would have to find a place where we could live with a greater deal of love from the people around us. When word came that I had got the first which everyone knew I would get and had on top of this got a Commonwealth fellowship to Manchester University, Machel hurriedly got in touch with some contacts he had at the music school there and secured a little teaching job. From the map which came with my offer of a place in the school, I saw that our schools were close by each other. We could share digs. And we couldn't fail to see from the note on demography that this was the place of multi-cultural, multi-ethnic and all the 'multis' you could think of. Our relationship was likely to be in the majority at last. I had never crossed the water, not even from Portmore to Port Royal by boat, and felt that I should not leave without this experience and Machel of course was ripe for any experience especially since he was leaving the Caribbean and its seas, so we bought ourselves tickets for a western Caribbean tour. He was not taking me. We were as usual two entities that happened to be going in the same direction.

There is not much you can hide if you live on campus in hall as I did. I was much talked about, not shunned and isolated. Anybody could come visiting and see my ticket on my desk. And I wasn't shy about answering. The whole world now knew that I was travelling on a Caribbean cruise and that Machel had a ticket too. "Honeymoon" they said. "What else we not hearing?" Weddings were on their minds. They had gone past showing their best profile and sending vibrations; they had caught their man and were into tying him down. Engagement rings and graduation certificate went hand in hand. Sometimes it was the wedding ring and the certificate, one ceremony after another – the gown and the veil following each other closely. I couldn't understand why anyone would be rushing to be in my mother's shoes or my father's for that matter. To be fair to marriage, I really did not have a wide range to look at. It was just that within my family and those of the mixed couples that I knew. None of them was as exciting as the not-marriage that I had.

It beat me for instance, that Valerie, with a good head in maths and fingered like me for a first should be rushing into marriage with Victor, when the only thing common between them as far as I could see was that their names both began with the same letter. Val was my good friend and we used to talk. She had looked at the field of metereology and had asked why there were only men dealing with the news about the weather. She had wanted to enter this field. When I asked why marriage rather than the excitement of learning something new, her answer was: "I won't take my youth and do with it what I can do at any other time." She could train as a metereologist at any time in her life, she was saying, but she had to be young to marry. I figured that marriage could come at any old time and you didn't have to give your youth to it. Machel had not asked me to marry him and I was not looking for that from him or anyone else, not when I could continue the study of Political Science at Manchester and perhaps have the great excitement of writing policy that could affect the whole world, the female Arthur Lewis or better than that.

Meanwhile Machel and I went unmarried on the cruise liner. There was precious little for two innocent children to do so we got to playing with our bodies. We had packed before and sent on our heavier luggage so all we had to do when we came back was get on a plane. That is what we did. I went on the plane to England without knowing what adult games had done to me. I arrived in England pregnant and unmarried. Sounds like the black story doesn't it? My family history came back to me and I have to confess I saw to it that Machel took care of himself and stayed alive for I did not want prophesy to fulfil on me and I become a single mother by a white man dead or alive. I have quietly had my daughter. My mother knows, in the way that mothers know everything. She doesn't care about the man, she writes. "Just bring my grand pickney mek me see it."

We are going to rustle up a wedding at the registry here and then come home for a short vacation. Even Machel's mother wants to know her grandchild. That's easier. We can do that over a weekend.

I don't remember who in the group had opined that Machel would have to impregnate me with his nose, and I don't want to know. I only hope it wasn't that person whom I hear is having to subject her black husband to expressing his semen so it can be determined whether his sperm count is low and can be helped by medical intervention. Cock mouth would really be catching cock and I don't wish that on any of us for we really had cared about each other if only in the first two years of living together and I do know that what seemed like anti-Machel sentiment was their idea of protecting me and getting me to be normal. Who's normal now?

Kishwana

For most people and it was so among the students at Grove High, Kishwana knew, the word 'shower' meant a way of bathing. You stood beneath a pipe which had a cross piece at the end of which was fitted a unit with holes in it and out of this came water. Or a 'shower' could refer to a shower of rain, rain falling in great drops suddenly. People with such understandings spoke of taking a shower as opposed to taking a bath, that is filling a container with water, sitting in it and with a rag, scrubbing your body as you scooped up water with the rag. There were no bath tubs where Kishwana lived. From time to time there were water lock-offs, announced if the company felt like being polite. On these occasions, you gathered water in buckets, one of which you reserved for your shower. This time the water would not come from a nozzle over your head. You would take a cup and throw water on your body from the neck down. This style of bathing was referred to more often as 'holding a fresh', a term which eventually also came to refer to what others called 'taking a shower'. When Kishwana heard the word 'shower', she expected to see not a way of bathing or a downpour of rain, but someone or some people dressed in green, quite likely holding the right hand aloft with the pointer and third fingers making a vee sign and shouting 'shower', which was a call for all in the yard to put on their green outfits and run to join those massing in the street.

Kishwana

Kishwana had been labelled as 'bright'. She knew that and she knew that that was why she was going not to the neighbourhood high school but to one to get to which she had to take a bus. She knew that her classmates didn't have this understanding of the word 'shower': they might know that the word referred to a particular set of people as well as a way of bathing or a downpour of rain, but they didn't know the excitement associated with it; how we walk around the area with branches of green trees that we break on our way, singing; how we collapse on the ground in the park and are served chicken and rice in little white covered boxes, served by people who look like they could be the parents of these children who are in my class, none of whom I have ever seen down my way. Arthur was one of those who took showers as opposed to taking a fresh. Of course Kishwana didn't actually know this, for he didn't live anywhere near her and she did not know anybody who knew him outside of school.

It was the habit of the boys in this co-educational school, to stand at the back of the assembly – boys were always in the lines at the back of the assembly. Why would the teachers keep on putting them there if they knew they would make noise and sometimes so much that whatever the occasion was for the assembly, it would have to be aborted. She didn't know whether he meant it or not, but out of the corner of her eye, she did notice that Arthur was one of those who made a joke of the Lord's prayer, pushing his fist up in the air and shouting "power" when the part about 'for thine is the power and the glory' came around. It mightn't mean anything too tough for most of the boys were doing that and she didn't think that they could all be from that party which shouted "power" at election time.

She didn't let that bother her. He was making her feel normal and that is all she could care about at this time when it was so important that a boy looked at you as if you were special.

At that school, people weren't hard up for money. If one girl said to the other that she had no money, she simply meant that she had no money 'now', for she had used off her pocket money or she had forgotten to ask her parents for money but this lack would be corrected by the next day. The people Kishwana knew, seriously didn't have money when they said they had none. It meant that there were no bottles left to be picked up and exchanged for money to buy a piece of salt fish and a bunch of callaloo to make the dinner. And this was not a lack which neighbours could fill and would be filled next morning. You might get a couple of dumplings from somebody's pot if you had no money to buy something for your dinner, or a few fingers of banana from somebody whose people in the country had sent up a crocus bag by the country bus. But that was it. People didn't play around with food either; they knew that a money value could be put upon the couple of dumplings that one gave another.

That is why it shocked her at first when the thing to do between boys and girls was for boys to come steal the lunch of the girl he liked. It was usually upper sixth boys who came courting lower sixth girls. That was the fashion. The boy might say: "Wife I come for mi dinner" and run away with what she was eating. Quite often, though, he would come back with a chicken dinner for her before the bell announcing the end of the lunch break rang. And this lunch would be in a box rather like that which people like her got only on the occasions when there was electioneering and they were running out to shout "shower" and settlings on the grass in the park and fed like one of Jesus's multitude.

This here at high school, was a charade between boys and girls, just a courting game with food made to behave like stoppers on a draft board – just swapping a cheese, chicken, beef sandwich, whatever, for a box of fried chicken which you *bought*. "Your hand sweet" the boy might say on his return and the girl would smile, though both, knew she was sure, that it was a maid like her mother who had made that sandwich and whose hand was really the sweet one.

She didn't have sandwiches in her lunch kit. And her lunch kit was a biscuit tin which her mother had got somewhere, she didn't know wherefrom and which used to keep eggs until her need for it became greater. It was not like that of her classmates. Theirs were plastic boxes; the sandwiches were wrapped in thick toilet looking paper or in shiny foil and the box had a place for a Thermos flask in which was a drink. These boxes had a hasp which was easy to open. Her biscuit tin was very hard to open, especially as it was now old and becoming rusty. No boy would see how to run away with that. And in it were usually a bit of what her household had had for breakfast – some leftover dumplings with callaloo or steamed cabbage. And nobody had prepared that for her. In fact she had prepared it for the whole family as she had been doing from age ten to her now sixteen.

But Arthur did take away her 'lunch box'. He had looked at the writing on it, called the name of the kind of biscuits which must have come with the tin and declared that these were his favourite biscuits. Had he been around her long enough, he would have realized that this was a 'lunch box', not a biscuit tin. And that people in her life did not know those biscuits. Kishwana just kept her cool. She didn't try fighting for her 'lunch box' like the others did, just part of the courting thing, for then you couldn't help being in the arms of the courting fellow. She only smiled as she anticipated the next act: Arthur's response to cold, old, fried flour dumplings with equally cold callaloo and salt fish.

The boy was a diplomat. It was that day that she really started to like him. No 'respect' was the better word. He came back with the usual chicken-in-a-box. Her fried flour dumplings were gone. He might have thrown them away but he certainly seemed to have eaten even one, for there was oil around his mouth and the smell of salt fish. Without the usual flourish of the courting male, and speaking unusually softly he told her: "We have a helper named Miss Eugenie; your mother's dumplings are as good as hers."

"My mother?" she asked just as quietly, though her voice was full of the surprise and annoyance she felt. "I get up at five o'clock in the morning when you just turning over for another set of sleep, to make these."

"Girl, I know you bright. I know that you are a maths whiz, but let me tell you, your dumplings are as good as your maths, if that is true," he retorted, really shocked. "What else you can cook?" he continued and without giving her a chance to answer, he said, "Hope you know that from now, your lunch have to share with me." Kishwana felt that she could now claim to have a boyfriend. The thought made her tremble for she never expected it; never planned for it.

She had been an observer in this foreign land, all the time, watching this courtship business. She knew it was a game and she knew she didn't know how to play that game.

Going to parties seemed to be a great part of it. The other girls talked about 'the parties they had gone to and who do you think was there? So and So; what I had worn, what So and So had worn and what do you think So and So said to me? And who do you think was with him or her and how do you think I felt?' She wasn't into that. Even if she had wanted to, where were the clothes and the shoes and bus fare for the party to come from? 'Bus fare?' These children didn't go to parties in bus. And who was going to stay with the children while her mother went off to her late shift if she was gone off to party? So she dismissed the whole boyfriend scene like a parcel which had come to the wrong address and picked up her books for the next class shortly after Arthur left for his classroom or whatever.

How did he come to choose her? Kishwana wondered although she had made up her mind that the parcel which came to her had been misdirected. She was 'bright', he had said. She knew she was bright but what had that got to do with 'love' and she hoped this was 'love', mainly because it was romantic to think so and why shouldn't she have romance, she thought to herself. Romance didn't have to be tied to action; it merely provided the basics for one to dream on. And the dreaming was better if the basics were real and true. It was not necessary for her to go to any party with Arthur or for him Arthur to take her to anything at all; she only needed to know how she came to be the chosen one, what about her had attracted a male person. That knowledge would bolster her self-confidence as a female person.

It was a question she put to Arthur in one way or another when she was quite sure that the relationship was consolidated, when the swapping of lunch was a regular and established event. What he told her didn't help her self-image very much. He knew her long before talking to her, he shamefacedly acknowledged to her. It seemed she didn't know how popular she was in her area or else his comment would not have been the let down he saw on her face, he had said. He told her in essence that he had a good relationship with his helper, Miss Eugenie. "What has that got to do with me?" she had asked him. "She talks about you all the time," he had said. And she had told him that she didn't even know his Miss Eugenie. That baffled him, she could see in his face, but he continued to tell her that he even knew how many brothers and sisters she had and where her mother worked, though he didn't remember her name. "But, listen," he had said, "I'll tell you her name tomorrow and you will see that I really know about you and that you are a famous lady. Who can resist having a famous lady as a girlfriend?" he had teased. The next day when he came for lunch, he just said, "How is Miss Babs?" That really shocked her for her mother really was called 'Miss Babs'. Then he moved on to educating her about herself. "You don't seem to know," he said, "that you are the best thing that has come out of your area and that everybody there owns you."

"So you like me because…?" And she had stopped to let him fill in the blank but decided to fill it herself: "because the blind people among whom I live, appreciate their one-eyed daughter for her 'brightness'."

He took a long time to speak but finally said, "I don't like to say things like this to you, but I have no choice: Girl, I wonder if you have a long mirror at home? You probably don't, for you would be able to see the coca-cola figure that I see every day whether I actually see you or not. I guess you really haven't seen yourself because if you had, you couldn't walk about with so little self-consciousness. And I hope what I have said is not going to cause you to walk around now and be looking at yourself like the rest of the lower six girls. But tell me Kishwana, don't the men in the streets in your area ogle you? That really bothers me. From what I hear, women are in grave danger in those areas." Kishwana could honestly say: "that's not my experience and you don't have to worry." It was true, the men and boys did not whistle at her or try to touch her and no don men sent for her. She knew these things happened, so she now had to think about why it didn't happen to her but to girls she knew who were far her inferior not only educationally but in looks.

This boyfriend and girlfriend did very little more than talk at lunch time and they seemed to be satisfied with that. They were the butt of much talking though – Romeo and Juliet, they were called. It was the guidance counselor who made Kishwana know how close they were to this Shakespearean fiction. Kishwana was quite familiar with Miss Jenkins and Miss Jenkins with her. As a girl who was coming from 'that part of town', it was Miss Jenkins' business to see to her smooth integration into the school. So from grade 7, Miss Jenkins had been in her life. She knew when her little brother Clyde was born; she knew when her mother stopped selling on the street and got the job as a ward maid; she could not help knowing when Kishwana went to the summer camp in Manchester for it was she who arranged for her to be sponsored. So it was not odd that Miss Jenkins would call her to her office and mention that she knew about 'the boyfriend'. But the way she did it! "Power wherefore art thou power. An 'ower' by any other letter would smell as sweet." She was so dramatic and so funny but she left no time for laughing. She moved into, "Did you know that Arthur's father was a candidate for the electoral division in which you live? Had he won, your boyfriend's father would have been the power representative for the division in which you live. This shocked her and she put up her arm and massaged her shoulders as she usually did when she was tense. Miss Jenkins said, "This is not intended to make you back off or anything like that; it is just that I think you should know and I don't know who else would tell you beside me. So I told you."

Of course she told her boyfriend of the meeting. And of course he fussed and fumed and said that what they had was their business and Miss Jenkins only wanted to break them up. As if in defiance, as if she had put forward a political programme for shower which she was defending, he gave out that he was his father's son, not his father but that he supported his father's political philosophy and even hoped to canvass with him in the next election, though they both knew there was no hope of winning that seat; that they would not give up because right was might and when and if his father passed on, if he was twenty-one plus, he intended to take up the mantle and to give power the victory. He had looked into her eyes as if to say, "Are you with us?" whereupon Kishwana had grabbed up her books and said, "I have to go home, Arthur. You know how much I have to do there." The next day the ritual of exchanged lunch took place as if that political sparring had not occurred.

One place that Kishwana and Arthur could go out together was the stadium to watch the secondary school football matches, the Manning Cup. Everyone in all competing schools could get free tickets and they both got tickets.

This was an extension of school. Their relationship had not got out into the open yet, they thought. But boyfriend and girlfriend sitting together for two whole hours, meant the occasional unintended holding of hands, smiling into each other's eyes, sharing a drink from the same bottle and there were people there from other schools, so someone from her area was bound to say, "You couldn't introduce me to your boyfriend," meaning "I know you have a boyfriend. I don't think that those who should know, know and I am the one who can give you away." Word was bound to get back to the area and it did.

When it reached her mother, Miss Babs, she didn't send her to her doctor as some mothers of lower six girls were doing, for the talk and the pills. Nor did she box her down like some mothers in the area do and Miss Babs' own mother had done. She just said, "Kishwana, you know how things go in this family and what and what leave for you to do." Which of course meant we have no money to give to gynaecologist or to buy pills and you can't make boy business hold you back for you are the father of yourself and your brothers and sister. That was all. Kishwana called this permission to have a boyfriend. Her mother did not comment on his being a 'power boy'. Perhaps that part of the news had not percolated down as yet.

November came and with it short days and the early fall of the night. They were at the stadium until night fall. Arthur informed her that there was no way she was going to go down into that area by herself at that time of the night. She facetiously asked: "Am I going to stay at your 'power' house instead of going home?" As if it had not been a joke, he seriously answered in the negative adding that he would instead be going home with her to her 'shower' house. A weaker 16-year-old or one who had had cause to really understand the social and political situation of the area in which she lived, would have been thinking about the violence to which he was alluding and been frightened. Kishwana said nothing. It wasn't so much her area that she needed protection from, she felt; it was the bus park. She didn't actually see the man running with the knife in his chest and eventually falling in the Jamaica National building as dead as dodo but the thought that she could have seen this, frightened her. True, twenty-five men had been killed in her area in one day. She hadn't been around for that but the thought had not frightened her for it was a popular event in her area and moreover you had a good idea of who would be killed and who would do the killing, the latter were often easily identified, often being in uniforms. The bus park was different: people like rice grains and she didn't know who would stretch out his hand and grab her. Uptown kind of frightened her for she didn't know when and what to expect of their violence. She had seen men in shirts and ties do mean things and neatly dressed young men did carry knives and whisper vulgarities in your ears. It was after dark in the bus park in Half Way Tree that bothered her, not her area. Bad things happened but she wouldn't focus on them. A little company to get through these things was nice. Uptown Arthur would do well if even just to see her into the bus. He wanted to do more, she would let him. So Arthur his school tie, white shirt, his khaki and his books went home with Kishwana.

He felt a part of things when she left him with the key in her one-roomed palace while she went for the children from the child minder and when she knocked and he had to let her in. He could see how much she had to do – heating the cooked food, feeding the children and preparing them for bed, washing the dishes, and felt called on to advise her that though he lived above Liguanea, it didn't mean that he didn't know how to do household chores for his mother was a 'liberated' woman or at least called herself so, and held the position that the birth pains she experienced with him were no more or less than those she had experienced with his sister and that like her he would have to do his bit in the house. His sister now out of the island and the house, and he the only child at home, he had better know that he was the dishwasher and floor mopper for though she did have the services of a helper, nobody had given her to her as a slave and if and when this helper was overburdened and took off, she was not going to be the one to peel banana and roast breadfruit which they all felt was necessary to their proper growth, so the house she ran had to be spic and span to meet Eugenie every morning and the men in that house had better know that nothing should be said or done that could caused Eugenie to give notice. Indeed, she was 'Miss' Eugenie for she was a big woman and that was all that qualified one for respect and titles.

"I bet you wash at a sink though," she teased him. "Tonight you wash the dishes in this plastic basin with water from this plastic pail and you are lucky that my mother drew this water before she left today or you would have to go to the stand pipe in the dark, battling with the frogs while you fill the bucket." The thought of having to go outside to find a pipe etc. did not fill him with pleasure and the thought came to him that he didn't see anything looking like a toilet attached to the room that they were in. He just hoped that nature did not call.

He noticed that there was a big bed in the room pushed

to the wall and some hardboard with foam on the floor. This latter Kishwana had pulled from under the bed after she came in with the children. It was clear that the little children slept on the floor. Kishwana was even then wiping them down like his mother used to do when he was much younger and had a fever. She was wiping the children with a rag dipped from time to time in a plastic container in which she had poured some water. Having fed them and given them water to swill around in their mouths and spit out, she was now putting on to them their version of pyjamas. The gargling exercise he assumed rightly, performed the function that his toothpaste and toothbrush would. But how did they manage not to spit on anyone when they disgorged the water from their mouths on to the outside, for Kishwana did not allow them to spit in the container which held the water which she was using to wipe their faces and their little bodies? Kishwana heard their prayers then spread a sheet over them and was ready to give a little energy to him, her guest.

He was curious about the sleeping arrangements for five people in a room which was no bigger than that which he occupied by himself. If someone had to step from the bed, how did they know that they were not stepping on the children. And what if anyone needed to go to the bathroom? He didn't see any chamber pots like were in his grand-aunt's house in the country. He knew he could ask these questions for Kishwana was not at all embarrassed by her lifestyle. She would answer him as clinically as if he had asked her a question in chemistry. It was he who was shy about asking the question because he was shy about the bed. Them together in a room dominated by a bed, was too much. "So while you are here who is washing the dinner dishes at your house?" she had asked, which made him realize that his mother must be having kittens now. He called her with his cell phone. Kishwana knew it was a popular item for stealing among the people with whom she lived, and she heard that he was invited to take a taxi home and it would be paid for when he was delivered. She let him out and worried about him and his cell phone, "I wonder if Arthur would be rash enough to be talking on his cell phone, perhaps phoning a cab while walking to the main street?" The other wonder, not a worry, was what Arthur and his parents would say to each other tonight when he arrived home from her house. She knew that he would share that with her tomorrow and she was eager to hear. This whole affair was better for Kishwana than *The Young and the Restless* which everybody down her way watched with bated breath, and like them she eagerly awaited the next episode but in her case, it was of the play in which she happened to be one of the principal actors.

Arthur's mother and father were up to greet him. They both confessed that they knew about the girlfriend but his father's further comments really shocked him and brought doubt for the first time to Arthur concerning his socialist stance. Mr Keiz took him aside to ask about condoms. He seemed quite shocked to realize that nothing had been done which required condoms. He couldn't figure out why his son would be risking his butt to go into that 'area' at this time of the night if he was not there to sow the wild oats which every young man of his class had a right to plant there. He was shattered: his father was no better than the guys in his class. His schoolmates' reaction he could better understand for he knew them to be shallow pleasure seekers. They assumed he had 'busted'. Of course in their case, the courting swap had long moved from food to what they called 'loving' and it was understandable that they should see his journey in the same way that they saw theirs. What was disturbing was that they had assumed Kishwana to be public property and been asking him for a piece of that action. Come on, the child was 16, a year younger than most of them. What qualified her to be seen as a loose woman? Arthur was now for them 'King Arthur of the Round Table'. Some pressure yes; but not more than he could bear. That his father could see a 16-year-old girl in the same light as these 17-year-old boys did, bothered him plenty and he wondered whether, should the occasion arise, he could leave Kishwana in his presence and be sure that he wouldn't make a pass at her. He had accordingly been rude intentionally to his father for the first time that he could remember. He had said to him, "She is my girlfriend, Dad. Accent on 'friend'. Ever had such a thing Dad? Not 'girl bought'. Sorry you don't know the difference."

His mother sensed that he was upset and came into his room. That lady whom he considered pretty odd but whom he dearly loved, came into his room whispering: "Grandfather Keiz had a women in the ghetto along with his German wife. Your father was the outcome. You never wondered why our family on his side is so small, no uncles and aunts? Forgive him. He doesn't intend any slight to your girl. That's the reality he knows. I would not be surprised if I had a fellow wife in some ghetto somewhere." He fell asleep wondering what this woman so happy to call herself 'liberated' was about to do about his business, for liberation meant for her, minding other people's business and solving their problems without being invited to do so. He was even more convinced that the ultimate physical connection was out for him and Kishwana for she clearly needed protection and that, even from him. At the lunch swapping time, he was there as usual. He was a bit quiet for he didn't know how to tell her what had happened at home without mentioning his father's reaction and his reaction to it. She bailed him out with her comment: "I enjoyed our closeness last night but if you think it is going to move into anything more physical, think again. My mother is a big woman and after her husband left five years ago, she has not once brought a man into the bed. Surely I can do the same." He did wonder how that would work: a man in bed with the two women. Would Kishwana be relegated to the floor with her sister and two brothers if a man joined the household? Instead of asking this, he replied to her speech: "And who is asking you?" She was unruffled, "Just wanted you to know my position" she said, "and I am mighty glad that you are not asking."

Who was to win the Manning Cup had done so, and who was to win the DaCosta Cup had also done so and all of Kingston's youths were getting ready to go down to the country for the first leg of the Olivier Shield. He was going of course and he did want to know if she would be going, but their conversation had thrown cold water on his enthusiasm and he walked away without asking. Just as he had not told Kishwana why he did not intend to push her into the final embrace Kishwana had not told him why the subject had been so close to the top of her head that day. As it happened, Miss Bertie, short for Bertinella, who keeps the children, was waiting for her as she left home for school to tell her that she didn't mind if she came for the children after the young man left in the evenings. She was bound to cogitate on what Miss Bertie expected to happen if the children were not around. She had and she had made her decision.

Meanwhile, liberated mother had been busy. "I know where Kishwana lives and I am going down to visit on Saturday." She was his mother and all that, and if the unimaginable did happen and there was a child, she would have to look after it, at any rate, he would want to take the burden and that did mean putting it on her, so he couldn't shout at her too loudly in his annoyance, but he did advise her that those yards with their many prying eyes was not something she would like, and in any case she was the wife of the 'power' candidate and surely she didn't want people to think that she was there for politics, so he had a better suggestion: invite Kishwana to visit you. I'll probably give up going to the country for the Olivier Shield and watch it on TV with you and Kishwana. Liberated mother did overdo things a bit. The invitation, it seems, went not just to Kishwana but to mother and the rest of the children.

Lunch was nice. Quite relaxed. Forks only, so no one had to bother about who knew how to coordinate knife and fork and who didn't. Feeling that he had his mother and her mother's blessing on their friendship, Arthur felt free to put his arms around Kishwana's shoulder and show her the house and put Clyde on his back on the way to helping him to use the toilet. A little plus here for Mrs Keiz was that she could ask Eugenie to join them for a meal as she had been wanting to do for a long time. Mrs Keiz had selected for herself one label only. It was 'liberated woman'. Her husband was the 'socialist' and she let him take the lead on matters of class and he had said that having Eugenie dine with them would be more stressful for her than it would be for them. He ought to know, she felt, but today was a woman's day and no one could tell her that Eugenie who knew Miss Babs more than she, the hostess did, would not be a credit to the luncheon party.

When Arthur finally got to view the film, *Slum Dog Millionaire* and saw the children walking through the excrement, his mind came back to this day and what he had thought of Kishwana: she could walk through heaven, hell or sewers with the same equanimity. In other words, for her 'everything' was indeed 'everything', as the current saying goes, for here was Kishwana taking in his parents' split level house as if it was no more than a one-room space in a tenant house in West Kingston – no oohs and ahhs – she was not fazed by his mother's wall of crystal nor his father's bound law books. Like she had lived it all before. His mother had taken to calling her Kish as her mother did. Her mother had not gotten to calling him anything; she was meeting him for the first time. They called them to join them, for the talk had moved around to their business and there were things they wanted to say before the telecast of the football match began.

"Arthur, you didn't tell me that Kish was doing some subjects in CAPE with your year," his mother said as if he had been in the habit of talking to her about Kishwana. He didn't know whether he was to unmask her or just react gently and try to be nice to her. He choose to try niceness and did so wittily.

"I have seen her enter our classroom at maths times but I didn't know why. I kind of thought that she was trailing me or that the teacher brought her in to throw our ignorance in our faces."

Kish could have told him that; she didn't have to be so secretive, he was thinking when his mother, bless her dear heart, gave out that they could help each other by studying together. Neither he nor Kish responded. "Let the planners plan," they seemed to be saying. Then his mother had a better idea: "If Kish could move from CSEC math into CAPE math so easily, then she is probably gifted. She should be interviewed by Dr Minott and his AQUEST." The liberated woman would arrange it. And she did. Now Kish was more often above Liguanea than in West Kingston. That's where the trouble started and Miss Babs felt called to action.

Miss Babs decided that she would go to Bellfoot Pants, the don man who, now that the long-standing MP had retired, was called 'caretaker' and expected to run and to win the seat in the next election. He was glad to see her and cleared the room of sycophants before he began. "Barbara," he said, he had always called her by her right name, pronouncing every syllable, for it, as he had said in the long ago, was a name he liked, "how you fi go tek Kishwana gi her 'way to uptown people. And not even uptown people, but 'power' people and worse of all to the man Keiz that is my opposition?" In their youth, Bellfoot had been that guy, considerably older than she was, who wore the bellfoot hipster and sported a big fat 'fro. Miss Babs and her friends had put that name Bellfoot Pants on him and it had stayed. So she said now, "Bellfoot, you never once deny that Kishwana is yours and you did come and say so when my mother was about to kill me with licks. And that is good. But you never once buy her a sweetie or a piece of hair ribbon. I know you never had it and that your ambition was politics and that take any little money you have for you always have to run boat for these people round you. I never feel any way, for me know how to make my own payday. When Cunningham come around and I married and started having children with him, you didn't feel no way that he was treating Kishwana like his own. You know how Cunningham died: a man of his age had no business in your group and getting himself killed in shoot-out with police. I didn't say nothing, though is me who had to find money to bury him and now have to take on more sessions in order to make ends meet for Kishwana and the children he leave behind. I know that as long as Kishwana is down here, not a thing or a person dare trouble her for they know what nobody don't tell them, that you will kill for her. But me don't want things to come to that. I suppose you know that she have boyfriend and you know who the boyfriend is."

"And you carry her gone up at his house gone sell her for lunch money," he broke in.

"Bellfoot," she said to him quietly, "What if one of your fool-fool lieutenant to curry favour with you, go trouble that boy! Star headlines: 'Power boy killed for visiting Shower girl'. You think your party going to confirm you and canvass for you? You well know sey all the big-ups in the party dem whether shower or power, the both of them live pass Liguanea, and go to the same church and drink champagne together."

"And I am not going to stop them from seeing each other. It never strike you that I follow through with the invitation to the Keiz to see how they feel about our daughter? Well is that. And the woman start to do for Kishwana what I cannot do and what I know you cannot do. You thinking bout clothes and lunch money. I not allowing anybody, especially the mother of my daughter boyfriend to suit her out in any clothes, for I know they will think they own her. Same reason I wouldn't let you buy me shoes, when you did want to and you could afford it. I never even ask you for anything for Kishwana much less take clothes and food from stranger. I thinking bigger than that. What they have and I will take from them, is contacts that can affect Kishwana's future independence. You know what a actuary is?" Bellfoot was quiet. "Is when I go up there that I know the name, only the word. All now I trying to figure out what actuary do. Well is that Kishwana want to be and the lady start make connections for her already.

"You know I don't have to tell you anything for your name not even on her birth certificate, but I telling you all the same. That uptown school where she is going think that she is very bright and instead of keeping her to do the next exam in two years time, she doing it in one year. The lady is organizing for her to have extra lessons with someone who, if she continue to do well, can train her for a scholarship to America to help her qualify and come back to Jamaica as an actuary. Mi know you don't pray, but pray for her all the same that she get scholarship. Neither you nor me would want to see her get hold back if she can go forward, so stop the foolishness." Bellfoot was already beginning to sit up straight and to square his shoulders as if to tell off someone. "My daughter is an actuary, and what is you? Talk bout!" The clincher came finally: "You know sey bad to bad mi nah vote for nobody else but you, so you nuh need worry 'bout that and you know sey Kishwana nah go turn into 'power' just so. We never even see the man Keiz. I even doubt whether the woman is 'power'. She call herself 'woman's lib' and I know sey women of all stripe is into that. When them having meeting on her verandah, I hear, them have power woman and shower woman and woman of all class and kind there drinking tea and lemonade. Bellfoot don't make problem where no problem exist."

Bellfoot was thinking, "A man like me need a good wife. I wonder if Barbara she would do? She really is a fighter and like how the two of us old now, the age difference nuh look too bad. And is true she don't really ask me for nutten. Not even for Kishwana, so she would be no more strain on me than she is now that we are apart. Wonder if mi shoulda go back and try with her?" And the other wonder was, how are people to know that Kishwana is his daughter if she doesn't carry his name and doesn't even know that he is her father. Barbara had let herself out and was gone while he was wondering, so that kind of argument would have to be put on the agenda for another meeting.

Kishwana did better than everybody else in the class although she was technically in lower six. Her boyfriend scraped through. There were several failures: CAPE maths is a serious thing and liberated woman couldn't give Kishwana enough praise for she could see her hand in her son's academic success. Of course she got the scholarship and instead of going back to upper six, went off to a small college on the East coast of the US where they specialized in the training of actuaries. Even now the boyfriend is trying to figure out whether liberated Mama intended to separate them or was just interested in the fortunes of another female. He had contemplated an engagement but she had said, "Give the child a chance. Let some air flow around her. You have been protecting her too long. Leave her to grow. If you are destined to be together, nothing will stop that." So he got a little job in a bank and spent time with his father working on his constituency.

Kishwana did not mind not being engaged; she did

want to feel the air flowing around her. It flowed around her fulsomely in the US for neither the men nor the women interested her and she spent her time with herself, distinguishing herself and for the first time earning a little money. The only attractive person was one of her lecturers. By chance they patronized the same lunch room at about the same time daily. He exposed her to all sorts of issues at the intellectual level which she either had not thought about or did not want to think about – kinds and qualities of wine, global warming, the Arab–Israeli conflict, male–female relations. The issue of sex of course came up. Intellectually. He told her that women are more likely to become addicted to sex than men; that though he was quite willing to induct her into this addicting art, he did already have someone whom he had sworn to try to satisfy.

Kishwana did not find this an attractive offer and telling herself that her boyfriend was after all hers and hers alone, concluded that if sex is this addictive thing, she would be better off getting addicted to her own than to a stranger who in any case already had a mate. Loneliness and the feeling that it was time for her to realize her woman-ness, made themselves into an airline ticket. Kishwana offered Arthur a holiday. Apart from everything else she was tickled pink that she 'from that part of Kingston' could be sending a ticket for him from above Liguanea.

The idea of the engagement came up. It would have to be a long one, she said for there were still her mother's children for her to help into the working world. A long engagement he saw as a wicked tease and was not interested in it. She didn't tell him this but she didn't see that he was economically ready for marriage. She did tell him though that his father's politics was foolishness and contrary to what he allowed himself to think there was no heritage there for him. Was there some course that he could study for at her university? She was quite willing to see him through school. Getting a job would be no problem for her and what she would earn there in the States would be enough for them to live on and for her to send home to her mother. Also she was about to graduate and this meant a much larger salary than she was getting now as a part time worker.

It was after he had got back home and discussed the matter with his mother and her mother that he agreed to take up the offer. Liberated mother said this was just the right way for them to seal their relationship for Kish was the kind who would feel that she owed the Keiz something and this way she would feel that she had discharged her obligation. This way she would be free even to leave the marriage if she felt like it and that is how people contracting a legal union should feel, no baggage taken into the marriage. So Kish came out and they got married. Her little apartment was to be both the honeymoon spot and the new home of the couple. He would be studying finance.

Bellfoot had been at the wedding. That didn't surprise her. He was now the MP for the area and those were invited everywhere, sometimes even felt they had a right to be invited and turned up without getting the formal invitation. What surprised her was Bellfoot and her mother whispering together with her mother saying something like, "Tell her if you want to." With her veil around her face, waiting for the limousine to collect her for the church, Bellfoot comes and tells her, "I am you Papa you know." She didn't know what to do with this. Her mother had never allowed the issue of "who is your father" to be raised. She knew she was only half sister to the other three children and she knew that their father had died in a shoot-out – she had been too young and perhaps too focused on other things to take him in in ways that would allow her to remember him, but she knew she did call him Papa and been satisfied with that. She looked to her mother but she only shrugged and lifted her eyebrow. All that came to her mind was: if this man is the MP surely he can afford to get someone to dress him – that blue polyester, probably built free by some sycophant, certainly would not do. Then the man said, "Me and your mother talking again you know. She don't tell you?" Her mother shrugged and raised her eyebrow again. A father and a husband on the same day! Then she decided to get tough: if he was looking to walk her down the aisle in his polyester suit, he could think again. And she said it as clearly to him as possible: "So that's why nobody troubled me when I was growing up. I thank you for that protection but it is Miss Babs and I who have been struggling together. I still want her with me as I walk down the aisle and to give me away for is she who really had me. I suppose given your political position, you will be on the list of speech makers."

When during said speech he said how proud he was of his daughter who was something he hadn't heard of before and was marrying into the opposition and would surely bring power into his shower, all knowing that Kishwana had grown up on the wrong side of town, simply thought that by 'daughter' he meant, a child of the constituency, for the nature of the paternalism there was well known. It was true though that he and Mr Keiz were moving towards each other but this had begun well before she had thought seriously about the marriage. She felt that they deserved each other: power in his shower and no doubt a showering of power. This daughter-in-law had always accused her husband and his father and her father of having political philosophies by network. She felt that neither of them even knew what their parties stood for and had simply put labels on themselves because they were in a network which sported these labels. Power in my shower and a showering of power, indeed. Her husband was going to study finance and she hoped she could steer him afterwards into law. That should be easy. "Don't you think you should follow in your father's footsteps and take up his profession?" is all she would say and hope that he could see this as a better salute to his father than that silly business of politics in which he was continually coming second, at any rate.

Kishwana's apartment had a queen-sized bed like the one in Miss Babs's room in Kish's school days and which had thrown Arthur into confusion. He had spent the first night of his first visit to her on her carpeted floor telling her that he wanted to understand by experience how bed people manage not to step on the floor sleepers. Some time near morning he saw a light in the bathroom: Kishwana had gone to the bathroom, stepping over him without turning on the light in the room. He had asked her how she managed it and been told that he had set up his experiment foolishly. If he wanted to find out how bed people managed, he would have to be bed people rather than floor people. The next night he was bed people and she floor people and he managed to get to the bathroom without turning on the room's light or stepping on her but she was awake and said to him, "so you understand about sensing presences now."

The following night he took up residence on the floor and begged to be washed down with a rag like she had done her brothers and sister and added that if he was to understand both sides of the story he would have to experience being the washer-downer as well. He got his experience and they liked it so much that they were both floor sleepers that night and both the washed and the washer. That brought them so close that the next nights all he had to try to understand was what it was like for a man and woman to be in bed and the children sleeping on the floor. Kishwana told him about Miss Bertie and that she was now ready to do what Miss Bertie had expected her to do if she kept the children until after her 'boyfriend' left. It was after these wonderings that Arthur told her that he was not into any long engagement, and it was reflection on what her lecturer had told her about sex and addiction, that had had Kishwana beginning to turn over in her mind how to have the man in the bed and still be taking care of her brothers and sister.

I had studied English literature from Chaucer to the Moderns. This was high school and of course like every other Jamaican girl I had read 'penny dreadfuls', and 'True story magazines' so I knew about love. I had read Spanish and Latin and therefore knew of the great love of Orpheus and Euripides, Anthony and Cleopatra as well as that of Romeo and Juliet, Elizabeth and Darcey, and Goya and the Duchess of Alba. I had soaked up love films, for Saturday evening matinee was my only pleasure and though I went for the 2:30 matinee I usually stayed over for the 4:30 one. I absorbed the love affair of Anthony Perkins and Joan Crawford in *Autumn Love*, of Deborah Kerr and Cary Grant in *An Affair to Remember*. I was always an observer except for the ill-starred love of Belafonte and Dorothy Dandridge in *Carmen Jones* and the little bit we saw of Sidney Poitier and Diahann Carroll in *Paris Blues*. People like me were rarely in the love scenes so when I met Maurice Bayley, I could not see it coming, could not see myself as a star.

Maurice was my boss's brother. I was eighteen. Just left school, finished A-levels just a few weeks ago and now was in the civil service. Freddie was head of my section and supposed to teach me the work and to supervise me. He managed to make lunch dates and picnics in the country, part of this and once even a visit to his little flat. It was while I was sitting down on his sofa, spotted as if a cat or some other animal had been peeing on it, that I saw the face of a man peeping out at me from what I assumed was the bedroom into which room Freddie had separated himself from me and gone. Then there were hushed voices – sounded like a quiet quarrel, then the fellow who was not Freddie, came out, told me he was Maurice, spelling it in what seemed an attempt to make me feel relaxed. "More rice, get it. The man who loves rice." He asked my name, my parents' names and other identifying data such as my age. Then he said he was going to take me home. He must have seen my surprise for he was particular to mention that he was at a divinity college training to be a minister of religion and was in a part-time job as a children's officer. He said my boss Freddie, his brother was not feeling well, had told him that I lived in the same vicinity as he and had asked him to "do the honours." With this last, he bowed and duffed his imaginary cap like the fool in a Shakespearan comedy. He opened the door of the little flat and ushered me out.

In his car which was a confusion of books and newspapers, nothing like the clean seats of his brother's, he continued to ask one personal question after the other about me. When we were about three quarters of the way home, he began to address me as Little Miss, letting me know that no job requires any boss to take me to his flat and that he hoped he never saw me at his brother's place again; that at my level and the tasks we had to do, I shouldn't be seeing Freddie more than between 8:30 a.m. and 4:30 p.m. He would suggest that I apply this to any boss but that he was laying down the rules concerning me and Freddie for Freddie was his brother and there was something called sexual harassment and that people seeing us so close could accuse Freddie of it and even I, could.

That seemed to be the end of Freddie and I for he was now very cold to me in the office and was paying attention to the newly arrived Cheryl. I go to Jesus Christ the Redeemer. Guess who turned up one morning as our guest preacher and who was to stay and do his practicum with us for six months? Freddie's brother. He could not help but see me for I was one of those placed behind the long tables to serve the lunch. He remembered me. "Little Miss," he said, "I am delighted that this is where I am meeting you again rather than in the place where we first met." I was serving the candied sweet potatoes on to his plate, when he remarked: "I am quite impressed with this place. Sweet potatoes served by the sweet." I was very much a part of the youth programmes so naturally we would meet on Mondays at these meetings. There were youths to counsel. Derek had been sleeping in the Sunday service. Was something wrong? Doreen had missed many meetings. We should check with her parents to see what was wrong. There were lots of chores to do together for I was in charge of the youth programme and working with the youth was part of his assignment. There was easy banter between us, and Mrs Brown with whom I boarded allowed him to come in and relax after the Monday sessions and always had a glass of lemonade for him, sometimes even a cookie which she had baked specially for him. After he had relaxed with his lemonade and cookie, we would walk back to the church hall where his car was parked, for there were always things of which to remind him or things he only now remembered that he should tell me. The first "I can't let you walk back alone," was said so often, he stopped saying it and I just got into the car now and was driven the little distance back to Mrs Brown's. She took to calling him my boyfriend and he to calling me "Little Bit."

Maurice might have heard Mrs Brown speaking of him in this way and wanted to make things straight. I don't know, but shortly after, he showed me a photograph which he took from his wallet. It was of a very nice looking lady, about his size which would be nearly six feet to my five foot four. He said she was his fiancée and she was studying nursing in Canada. The introduction of the girlfriend changed nothing between us; she being in Canada and we still having our youth work to do, him to relax with lemonade and our minds to forgetting this and that and having to walk to the car and drive the little way back to my home. Then about three months later – it was near to Christmas – he handed me an envelope which had several other envelopes in it. It was addressed to me. I noticed the letters RSVP at the bottom of one of the cards. I knew what it meant but had never been asked to RSVP before. I was thrilled and smiled at Maurice who just stared at me and said, "But you haven't read the invitation" and continued staring at me. I read it. It said "Mr and Mrs Charles Benbow, request the pleasure of the company of," and my name, "to the nuptials of their daughter Thelma Elaine to Mr Maurice Bayley."

"That's you," I said and added foolishly, "I didn't know your Bayley was spelt with a 'y'."

"Of course," he said, as if he knew my real question which was: "Are you really getting married?" and I suppose to all the questions written in my face, which face began to fall and he saw that I was about to break down, so he quickly said, "Come for a drive with me," shouting to Mrs Brown that he was taking me away for a short while.

He drove all the way to Morgan's Harbour and I sat

beside him without a word passing my lips. He parked and said, "Now we take a walk along the beach. He shepherded me out of the car and kept his hand around my waist while we walked. At a point he showed me the sunset, it was really beautiful and before I knew what was happening, I was in a movie, I was having my first kiss. It was as long as that in *The Wind Cannot Read*. And after that there were several others on the same walk. He told me that he loved Thelma and that they had been planning marriage for a long time but that didn't mean that he didn't love me. Not to worry, he said, things had a way of working out and quoted something that seemed like a Bible verse: "All things come together for those who love God." There was no need for me to be sad, he said. I wasn't losing him. We just have to be careful for some prying eyes could make a beautiful thing into rags.

When we reached my home, he sought out Mrs Brown. I heard him telling her that he had just told me of his forthcoming wedding and hear the lie, "She took it like a trooper. I had feared that she might have mistaken the closeness between us for more than it is and could be, but I had nothing to fear; she has never seen me as anything but her co-worker. "Perhaps I should even feel slighted, eh, Mrs Brown? A handsome man like me and this girl doesn't even fancy me?" One of the few West Indian writers that I read who deal with love and sex was Edgar Mittleholzer. In one of his novel, I don't remember which, there is some young woman putting some man's hand on her breast. I could not then for all the world understand why she would want to do that and why she and he would like that. I didn't see that in any of the films I watched. Maurice Bayley and I, in his book strewn car had moved from the lips to other parts of the body and I could now empathise with Mittleholzer's character. He always ended these sessions with "We can't go there." Where was there?

Thelma was coming for Christmas but that didn't stop our kissing and cuddling. It seemed the thought of Thelma would send us into more physical contact, some of which couldn't be helped for we were rehearsing for the Christmas concert. Along with all of this new territory were new questions of an intimate nature from Maurice Bayley: "Did I know of the term 'safe period'?" When I didn't, he gave me a biology lesson, got certain information from me and told me what was my safe period. One evening he said to me, "I want to honour you and our love" and drove me to a house which he said was his family home but no one was living there now except him. He took me to what he said was his room and had been from his earliest days. It was very clean and orderly, unlike his car, with white sheets and white pillow cases. He did a mock wedding ceremony: "I, Maurice Bayley, do take you Little Bit Curry." That was where the ceremony ended and the kissing and the touching took over and went on until we had disrobed each other. When he was ready to take me home, he said he was sorry that my honeymoon had been so short but he would make it up to me. Maurice did something I still can't fathom: he scooped up the sheet and said he wanted to launder them himself.

I still can't believe that Mrs Brown did not know what was going on or that nobody in the church community knew. I guess they must have thought that a female who was helping a man to find, furnish and tidy the house for him to live with his wife could not be in love with him. Only to Deborah Reynolds in *Tammy and the Batchelor* could anything like this happen and we know that she was a silly young country bookie, not even having seen herself in a mirror in all her fourteen years. Why Thelma didn't stay at our honeymoon house was left for me to guess. Her parents lived out of town, so for the week before going home and the weddings, she naturally wanted to spend some time with her husband-to-be in Kingston and with him to see to last minute things concerning their life together. She was also wrapping up a contract with the University of the West Indies Hospital for a post there. Maurice and I had been very detailed in our work on her behalf. It was my pleasure to be with him choosing furniture. Even the bedside clock-radio was my choice. It somehow was very important to me that he buy the miniature cuckoo clock. I insisted and he did buy it. And guess where Thelma would be staying for the days in town? She would be boarded at Mrs Bown's. Who could guess the true nature of the relationship between us three. Not those people who wrote love stories and filmed them, for I have never seen this theme in any of them – film or books.

I went with him to the airport to collect Thelma. She came to me as soon as she saw me, saying: "So this is my little sister. Thank you. Maurice has told me how hard you've been working to help him in his ministry and even in his private life, trying to fix up the house for us and so on." Maurice did not stop visiting Mrs Brown's boarding house. Of course there was no smooching with me then. There never had been at Mrs Brown's house any way. There was none with Thelma either, though Mrs Brown did tell him and he had exercised the option, that he could visit with her in her room. We still went for drive outs, though I was now in the back of the car.

I was at the wedding as bright as any corn seed and when it came to the vote of thanks, the groom singled me out as one to whom he had to express his gratitude on behalf of himself and his wife, for my selfless help towards their settling in and Thelma in her white dress hugged and kissed me before she went off to change for her honeymoon. It was not in my honeymoon house. It was further away on the North Coast. I hear that where people go for their honeymoon is a private matter and you are not supposed to ask them. I didn't ask. Maurice told me, and I chose to see a message in that. I stopped seeing Maurice Bayley regularly. There was a lot to occupy me, I was getting my things ready to go up to the university to do my bachelors in psychology. I had to see to taking the entrance examination and that involved a lot of running around – getting recommendations, getting my details from the Overseas Examinations Office, getting a medical test and so on.

Within months I had moved from Mrs Brown and away from Jesus the Redeemer and the youth organization, to live on campus. The Bayleys as they were now called, were very busy too for I only saw their backs at church or heard his voice on the few occasions that I could make it back to my church. They knew where to find me though for Maurice Bayley came to see me shortly after I settled in. It was in September. He came to give me the good news: "We are having a baby." I said I was happy for Thelma and he pointed out to me that he had said "We" and that included me for this was as much mine as anybody else's, no name called. I noticed that I was no longer Little Bit. It was never my legal name Lilieth, anyhow. Seems there was some paganism associated with that name so I was Little

Miss, then Little Bit, this last he liked best for it was an honest name given my size. I was now 'darling' whether as an honorific or whatever else they call what comes after your name. 'Little Bit darling' or 'Darling Little Bit', sometimes just 'Darling' were my new names. I asked about this name change and was told what a lucky fellow he was. He had two darlings. I had heard about Marcus Garvey our first national hero having wives of the same name and remembered someone saying how convenient. He could never slip and call the wrong name.

It was while on campus that I knew jealousy. I watched couples going to the union together to drink coffee, to dance or just hang out, walking off to the chapel gardens to do what Maurice Bayley and I used to do at the seaside. Where was my man? Young men came to try with me but I couldn't. I felt as married to Maurice Bayley as his wife Thelma was, and just to sit under the trees at daytime with some male and talk foolishness made me feel adulterous. Still my best friend, I confided word of these feelings to Maurice. He was pleased with my reaction. But I was angry at the situation especially as I didn't feel that I could talk to my new friends about my relationship. I felt like such an oddity. I was not able to enter into the man-woman discussion. Fellows in one hall, tired of being brushed off by me for no reason that they could see, me not being able to say that I was married to a married man took to circulating rumors that I was a lesbian. I was getting angry at the situation and it was not a happy part of me that went to see our baby, our son that Thelma had just pushed out that morning.

Maurice Bayley was asking me as he drove me to the hospital about names, for of course my suggestion is as good as anybody else's. I was in jest as well as in dare proffering such name as Zephaniah, Ahasusarus, Sunday when he asked me to be serious and I said, "What is all this bothering about? You know that his name is Marurice Bayley the second."

"That is his name," he said in the tone of voice that John the Baptist's father must have used on a similar occasion. I asked him what would have been the name if it had been a girl. He was ready for that. "She would take Thelma's mother's name officially but she would be called as I call you, 'Little Bit'." We arrived at Andrews Hospital in silence. I think the whole of Thelma's village must have come to worship the Christ child for there was a crowd of obviously rural people hanging about in the corridors and eliciting a bow of recognition from the proud father. At the door to the room, I froze. I still don't know why. Thelma was on the bed, her belly still big. I hadn't realized that pushing out the baby did not involve pushing out all that had made you fat. Later I realized that I hadn't even thought of Thelma in bed before. The Christ child was in a rectangular box beside her. For some reason, I could not walk in, and the father had to nudge me. But I crossed in front of him and walked towards the back of the room and through the crowd of more country people to a chair I saw on what was a small porch. I sat there until Maurice Bayley came sulking for me. "I am shocked," he said. "Perhaps I have been asking too much of you." But I got no time to respond for the bevy of country folk were around him and he was eagerly telling the story of the birth for he had been in the birthing room with her and had held her hand all through it. It was after they left that I got attention. "I had better take you home," he said.

I was skirting the floor, avoiding the bed when Thelma called me. I must say that he tried to give me a subterfuge: "She will miss dinner if I don't take her back now," he said. It was I who moved closer. She held my hand and kissed it. I took this to mean that she had noticed my reluctance to push myself into the holy family, had taken this as my new efforts to evaluate our relationship, was now seeing it in a negative light and she wanted me to know that she supported me and was encouraging me, for only I could reduce the triangle to sensible proportions. The husband whom I told this on our way home, disagreed. "There is no distress to her. She hasn't lost anything that she should get." I didn't even bother to say sarcastically what I was thinking, "Yes. You are right. It is she who has the baby, the house, the loving etc. and what have I?" Had I given voice to these thoughts I would have heard that the baby is mine too; that he has kept our honeymoon room sacred and that the house in which they now lived has more memories of me than of anyone else, no name mentioned. Did I forget that we had furnished it together etc.? I ought to know that every second that that clock signals reminds him of me; it was I who chose that clock. I just said nothing.

The reverend, for he had graduated from divinity school and had his own church, as he had learnt my menstrual cycle, had also committed to memory my work schedule. I go to August Town to do my bit of church outreach on Thursdays. One Thursday, on my way home I saw the reverend's car parked near to the old bus in which my group of youths meet. He was coming toward me with a bundle in his hands. It was Maurice Bayley, the second. I was about to ask what he was doing in these parts and with the young baby, when he said that they had come to meet me. He drove me to my hall with the little baby in his basinet and walked up the stair behind me, he with our baby now in his arms. "It is the time Little Bit, my darling," he said as I opened the door. "For what?" I thought but said nothing. He continued: "I have arranged with Thelma that she can work two sessions on Thursday, for you and I can keep the baby on the afternoon of that day. It is so convenient. I can drop her up to the hospital and then just come down here to collect you from August Town and take you and the baby to your room."

I said to myself, "Many of my fellow students do babysitting. They are asked to and they select a time as they see fit. And they are paid. Nobody has asked me to babysit, much less offered a fee." With that I started to understand my discomfort with this situation. It is that I am seen as an apostrophe. Having no existence except in so far as these people need me. I said nothing. Maurice loved me. Loved the fact that I was available, I saw. "Take your son," he said, and tried to put the baby's little arms around my neck. Had he not been holding the baby's bottom, I shudder to think what would have happened for until now I have not released an arm to hold it and the floor of the room is tile over concrete and not even a carpet to soften the fall. At this, the reverend Maurice Bayley became very annoyed. "This is my sperm," he said as the priests in the Anglican church to which I go on campus say, 'This is the body and blood of….' in a voice meant to brook no opposition. "You love me, love my sperm. What is so hard about that?" I said nothing and he continued: "If this place was a little bit more private, Maurice Bayley the second would be party to the honeymoon I promised you and he would see that you and I are truly joined." "But," I broke my silence,

"You no longer know my safe days." I was intending to draw attention to the fact that as far as I could see, we were no longer intimate. But he took another tack: "That body is mine" he countered in a now reasonable voice, "I know its inner workings and if I set myself to it can know what state it is in without doing any calculations." This was high science. There was nothing I could say so there was nothing I did say. I continued to say nothing until Junior and Senior, the first and the second, left with Maurice saying: "You are this child's godmother. You can't get out of that. I will tell you when the christening is. Let's see you deny him and me before the font of the Lord."

Then I had a long question and answer session with myself. What was wrong with the relationship? Was it even a relationship? What was a satisfactory relationship. I had new friends whose boyfriends who had boxed them, girls who had spent the night in my room crying because of what the boyfriend had done to them. Maurice hadn't really done me anything. Ah. I found it. I had no one to take me to the Union or to a dance. I know that if it meant that much to me, Maurice would have taken me. Then I switched to another thought for I needed to know why I felt so wrong. Maurice had never had to consider taking me to any place really for I hadn't wanted to go to any place any more than I now wanted to go to the Union or to a dance. "That is it," I said, "I don't now want to go to the Union or to a dance and I never wanted to go anywhere else but on church business or his business which we could do together, but suppose the day ever came when I wanted to go to the Union or to a dance, could Maurice really go or would he have to bend or twist himself into a shape that would allow him to go?" The conclusion came, "I am young. I will grow. Can Maurice really grow with me?" The answer was "No;" but was this because there was Thelma. I was thinking that Maurice, Thelma and I had been to several places together. Then it struck me that it always was places that one of them and very rarely, I had wanted to go. Suppose it was a place that only I wanted to go?"

I had help with my reasoning from an unlikely source. I was crossing the road to go sit under the big cotton tree to continue my reasoning with myself in more cool conditions when I saw Freddie. I didn't even know that he was a student on campus. As he later told me, he was sent by his agency to do a course in public administration. He wanted to know if he had just seen his brother's car pass. I told him that he had and he said "My brother is something, you know. He must really have God with him rewriting the rules for him for isn't there something called adultery. I am not too surprised at you for you are an innocent, experiencing your first bout of love but how does his wife go along with this? He has the big and the little of it."

At an earlier time I would have said, "With what?" and describe the relationship which certainly for the past year or so was nothing that the head of the church could not see. But this time I said: "Who says she does?" By which he knew I was answering his question about Thelma, for by now I was convinced that she found our relationship too close and was dying for it to die.

"I can see that you want an end to it," he said. Then seeing that our talk was in the middle of the road, he in his car and I leaning on it, he motioned me to one of the kiosks. He went to park and when he returned we sat and talked and talked and talked. "Three years!" he remarked. "Time for graduation." Freddie knew so much. I wondered how many more people knew as much as he and had chosen to shut up. "God is with him" he repeated "for I can't believe that the church people don't know what is going on. Or should I say what has gone on?"

"Yes, the latter" I said.

"Let me warn you," he continued [were these brothers born so that they could warn me against each other?], "breaking up will be very hard for him. You see he has nothing to lose and I am sure he can't even imagine why you would want to take a cookie away from him. I know a way," he continued, smiling, "though I doubt you will take it."

"Shoot," I said. He shot: "Remember it was I who first saw your beauty of form and spirit. Take me on."

"You are right," I said, "I won't take it. Is my world so narrow that there are only two brothers in it?" I asked myself and him, and my answer came back: and I spoke it aloud "There are millions out there. For Christ's sake, I am at the University of the West Indies. Not only is it supposed to have the best minds with the best opportunities for success but it serves the West Indies, not just Jamaica. So the best minds of about eleven territories are here, not to mention those who come on exchange from Europe and America. Can't I get one companion out of this number? Last time I looked there was no tree growing in my face. I must be able to get out of the Bayley family. As a matter of fact," I said to him, "Goodbye."

"See you at the christening," he said.

And I was there as godmother after all. In their system, a male child had two godfathers and one godmother. It is reversed if it is a female child. I was therefore the one godmother to Maurice Bayley the second. The father had called to tell me the details of the christening and asked when he should collect me. I was glad to be able to ask him then if any one minded if I took a friend who could also provide me with transportation. His 'that's alright' was very pale, but he brightened up with: "Little Bit you know I am responsible for you. Yes. Bring the fellow let me cross-examine him." Carlos was there to see me do my godmother thing. Out of the many suitors I chose him. He was not even from the West Indies proper, he was from Guyana, so I hadn't even begun to make use of the offerings of the University of the West Indies. After Guyana, it was Trinidad and back to Jamaica. Maurice Bayley first and second as well as Freddie Bayley and Thelma Bayley are more or less out of my life though I do go to birthday parties and take gifts at Christmas for the Christ child.

Thelma at the first of my post-break visits was very distant with me. She couldn't help but know that her husband was not visiting me anymore, that there had been a break and she could do the math, if there is a break there must have been something to break, a relationship, and she seemed to be having a late reaction to the fact of that relationship.

Nothing was ever said between us about it but soon her lively smile was there again. Given her size, her pregnancy hardly shows. It was showing now so she must be far along. It is this one that I thought of as mine for had my room been private enough, I cannot swear that the sperm which I think entered her at about that time, would not have reconnoitered in my passage and found itself an ovum. A tiny baby for those huge people, she deserved her name 'Little Bit' and so she was called. Nobody tried to put Little Bit's arms around my neck. She and I did that.

I was visiting one evening when I lifted up this little thing in her pink all-in-ones and put her little arms around my neck. I was singing and jigging with her when she looked into my eyes and laughed. Laughed. Her father looked up from the newspaper he was reading and her mother from the hemming she was doing. They both said: "This is her first laugh." I looked at her again and her face had gone neutral and blank as if a soul had left and the other had not yet taken its place. Maurice might have seen it too for I heard him say what I had once heard him say, "All things come together for those who love God." I realized then that Little Bit was really mine as I had thought and that he too knew it. I realized that I had guessed the sequence of events right. He had gone home from my room that evening very sad and Thelma in trying to comfort him – she understood the mechanics of our relationship better than we did – had got him to release in her body an essence that had been meant for mine. Thelma had allowed my baby to gestate within her. She had played the surrogate and I had no doubt that she knew it.

There was an unmistakeable bond between Little Bit and I. I wasn't embarrassed when one of the parents pointed out to me that I was Junior's godmother, indicating that I was not giving him as much love as I was giving Little Bit. And the little boy was quite cute! He was just beginning to lisp words and would climb into my lap and say, "Mother" whereupon one of his parents would remind him, "Godmother." Could I escape the Bayleys? Certainly not the Bayley children. This love was my choice this time. I wanted to love them. Was this romantic enough for English Literature or American films?

Lily

I had to hurry my exam to be home for five o'clock to let Basil in. I had had to shorten my preparations for my exam in order to tidy the place and get in some vegetables and tofu for him. He was a picky eater. He was moving towards Rastafarianism. My parents were not enamoured with him but sensibly said that I was a big girl. I am on time; Basil gets in on time but tells me he is staying with Novar who goes to my college and lives a couple streets down from me. What's going on? This is the fellow I have been with for what seems like thirty years though we are only twenty and twenty-one. We have been together since seventeen and eighteen and been planning marriage for just as long. Basil doesn't want to spend the night with me for he wants his head clear when we meet at breakfast to talk things over. What is going on? I know that he hasn't been doing very well. His grades aren't good enough to get him college funding and so he has to work and study, a situation which should not be visited upon a weak student for working doesn't give you enough time to study. But what to do? There is no money at home in Jamaica to help him. I hope he has not decided to drop out for at home without a degree, our goose is cooked. How will we get the mortgage that every newlywed needs? I am preparing myself to make the arguments against dropping out.

After a choppy night for me, the morning and the breakfast come. And Basil begins to present his case by leafing through his wallet for a photograph which he slides over to me. It is a picture of him and someone else. He is dressed conservatively, in a pullover with the collar of an inside shirt sticking out and a tie looking like a college tie. He looks like Harvard or Eton. Certainly upper class white.

"What is this?" I ask about the picture, feeling cold.

"This is Gerda," he says.

"And who is Gerda that she is the first item on our agenda?" I ask.

"She is our agenda" he tells me.

"How?" I ask, my heart now stone cold. Then he tells me that he and Gerda have been working on the school magazine. I want to say something facetious like, "So?" Or, "I am glad that your grades have so improved that you can hold a job and give time to the school magazine." But I shut up and watch him hemming and hawing.

"We get along very well," he says, "and we think we should give our partnership a more personal agenda." I listen and re-examine the photograph.

"She is white," I say.

"I know," he says, "but if you think we have suffered, you should talk to her."

"You have always been against black men marrying white women. You had a lot to say about my uncle who did this. You virtually destroyed him for me."

"I have learnt," he says stroking his chin, now hairless perhaps because of Gerda, "that there is one race. It is called the human race."

"So where has all this talk of Garvey gone? One race eventually, but in the meantime we have to secure a place in the world for ourselves. None but ourselves can free our minds."

"But Lily," he counters, "Nobody put a date on 'eventually'. I think it is here." I look at the picture of him and Gerda, two peas in the same section of the pod, his hands on her shoulder, she dressed in the same pullover, same tie and collar peeping out. I look at Gerda's hair, straight and flipped; at his smooth face and low cut hair and I see red. I see my own clipped afro and I think of my mother twisting her fingers to oil, brush and plait mine until it reached where with chemical straightening, it could be the length of Gerda's and flip and shake like hers. I remembered the early days of the romance when in high school uniforms we followed the university students to the prime minister's house. I remembered Basil pointing out their afro styled hairdos and telling me that this was the conscious style and how he loved it; how he had put his nose in my hair, kissed it and said, after I had cut it down right to the roots where the straightening had grown out, "This is my lady. A natural beauty." But the new lady can go off to the hairdresser and get her hair to flip and still be seen as natural – these stupid men think is only black women who need makeover and go to specialists for that. I put my palm over the photograph, still between us, bend my fingers and keep on bending until the photograph is crushed, breaking in some parts.

"Lily," he remonstrated.

"Who is that?" I asked him. "You forget that the name Lily was too Eurocentric and you had found somebody to rename me Abena? You fraud. I am only not spitting on you because white people are all around and I don't want them to observe black-skinned people fighting each other another time. Why did they stop lynching people like you?" I said, "I wish they would cut off your balls."

"Lily," he said again, "this is not forever. Gerda doesn't even know how her parents will take us but we think that in the interest of progress we should take a try."

"Whose idea is this, half-idiot?" I asked. "Has to be the white lady's, Bigger."

"Bigger," he muttered as if he once knew a Bigger but couldn't find the memory.

"You wouldn't remember," I said, "that's why you keep failing that course. Hope she helps you to remember. But just tell me this, "Why am I being asked to sit here and watch the black man I thought I was engaged to, tell me in the 1970s with black power all around us, that he is going off with a white woman? Where are the dashikis you came up with? And what's happened to your hair? It came up soul. If you wanted to make a change, couldn't you wear a ponytail like the Puerto Ricans or plaits like the fellows at home. Oh. Gerda doesn't know how to plait and in any case you don't want to look too political, she might feel threatened."

"You always were bright Lily. She doesn't know how to plait this kind of hair."

"So your girl children will be running around with their red knotty hair uncombed like those half Nigerians we saw and bemoaned in England last year?"

"You are going too fast Lily." With that I threw the crumbled photograph to the floor and ground the heel of my boots into it. I was turning to leave when he snatched my hand with "I'm surprised at you, Lily. I thought you were more liberal."

"My liberality does not stretch to fools," I said and yanked my hand away. "How does somebody who once looked like Walter Rodney chose to change to look like Prince Charles?

And did you tell her that you had retrieved your day name, that you are Kwashee with the short 'a'? No, you did not, for you really know that you are Qwaashe with the long 'a', you damned Quashee."

It was after I had got through the double glass swing doors that I broke down in tears, so blinded that I had to sit and cry them out before I could go on. Who should pass by but Joe Pangelleti from one of my classes. Really nice and popular fellow. One of the few of either sex who treats me as if I exist. Pity he comes in that colour. He came over, sat on the bench with me, put his arms around me and said the usual, "It can't be as bad as all that." I turned my head into his armpit and cried and he smoothed my afro with his hands like I suppose he does to his cat at home. I quickly regained composure, thanked him and was walking off when the swing door let through the dog. He had seen me in Joe's arms and looked surprised, even jealous as if to say: 'I caught you, you fraud. Your attitude is pure sham'.

"There is one race my friend," I said to him, "Meet Joe. He is of the human race."

I went home to my little room intending to grind all photographs and other mementoes of Basil under my heel but there was the smell. I had to understand the strange smell in my room first. Then I found it. It was a smell you get in the elevators, the toilets and all closed spaces. It was the 'white smell'. But what was it doing in my room? I was in Joe's armpit.

I went into another fit of crying. How can he give up my smell for this 'white smell'?

After Basil, I dated no one. I went out occasionally with men of all kinds – any man. I even spent some time with Novar, Basil's friend. He tried to comfort me and hoped that this break up would not undermine my womanness. I turned that womanness into yoga, into floral arrangement, into singing. My academic work was under no threat so I could afford to expand into other and unrelated fields. I came home with a good academic record and a wide variety of hobbies. It was just as well for on the campus that I now taught, there were hardly any available men, just more Basils than I cared to see. Alone again. Naturally. I would have to entertain myself, be my companion and best friend again. Such unhappy white women and such slap happy white men soaking up the local culture of calypso–reggae, sunbathing and beautiful black girls in tow!

Marilyn, the wife of Jeff, my department head, took to talking to me. She wanted to know why I wasn't married and why I wasn't running after one of the available men, black or white, married or unmarried. She was looking for company, hoping to drag out of me the kind of data which could have her say to herself "black women are unhappy too" and be comforted by that. I didn't cooperate. I just said, "Marilyn, I am a serious black woman."

"What does that mean?" she asked.

"You can't know," I told her, "for you are not a black woman." Then she got into the old Basil refrain, 'one race called humanity'.

"I'm glad to hear that Marilyn," I said to her, "so it won't bother you again when you see Jeff with...." Marilyn is a white woman and they are accustomed to having the last word so she didn't see my comment as 'Butt out and leave me alone'. She persisted, "But that's the point. If they did believe as I do that there is only one race, they would understand that it hurts to see them arm in arm with your husband in the SCR, both of them giving just a glance in the corner where we white women sit with a 'which-one-of-those-whimps-keeps-his-house-tidy' question in the glance." With that pain expressed, I sat to real conversation with Marilyn in which she offered two pieces of information which I would not have imagined. (i) She didn't want to choose the lesbian route. Other spurned wives like herself were pleasuring themselves with each other but here were jealousies, fighting and bitching so much so that she could not see this alternative as better than heterosexuality. (ii) Others had found a black lover but that's the kind of thing you do in college. She was a big woman and didn't intend to play that game.

"So what do you do now, Marilyn?" I asked, "Just sit in the white woman's corner and watch your man go by?"

"That's about it." she said. Then I told her about the history of white men/black women relationships and the resulting brown children very often distressed in one way or another and informed her that there was a children's home devoted to the offspring of these jokers and that she could be of some use if she volunteered to help there. This went well and others joined her to the point where they were raising funds and organizing scholarships for these children. Next thing was that they were forming themselves into a University Wives Guild. They wanted me to join it. I was happy to point out to them that the guild was for wives; this required husbands. I had none. I was let off that but not off my male colleagues' anger, for they missed having a wives' corner to humiliate and a sulking wife to dust the furniture and clean the floor and it was my fault that their wives had found something to do with their unappreciated time.

"It is your fault," Jeff said, "Now even our black girl

friends are being unionized. You know Celine, that I go about with?" he asked.

"Can't help but know her," I said, "the only place she doesn't go with you is departmental meetings."

"You would think so," he said "but now she refuses to go to the house with me although we know that Aldine is not likely to be there, she having all but moved in with Yvonne. I don't know where she got the word – perhaps from you. She is not a 'house frau', she says. So the house is untidy and the dust, I think is messing with my sinuses. She has also let me know that she has no intention of marrying me and that I am to make sure that my wife does not leave me. Once she would even pick up the children for me. Now she won't. Doesn't want anybody to think she is a maid or my wife. I can't make out which. You know that Sam has a situation like mine, though not altogether like for he is native, but his girlfriend is treating him in the same way. It is an anti-man thing not an anti-white man thing. What have you got against men, Lily?"

"Did you say Sam is feeling it too? Good for him" I said. Having met Sam's wife and remembering my own early situation, I added, "I wish his girlfriend would spit on him." I intended it as a kind of joke, something he could see as an exaggeration but the social psychologist chose to see it as gospel and wanted an explanation.

"But Celine is not to spit on me? How come? I am getting jealous, if not paranoid. Who is to spit? The wife or the girlfriend? I can't figure out whom you hate more, the husband or his girlfriend?"

"Ask Sam." I said to him and added, "Jeff, you are not really on my mind at all." The stupid ass did go to Sam with my comment with the result that Sam and I began having conversations, more like therapy sessions really. Sam has become that creep, Basil. He invited me out for further conversation.

"Not a date-date you know Lily, and Pinya will know that we will be going out together whenever we are. I know that is important to you." Her name was Espinet but her pet name was Pinya. I was sorry for her. 'Pinya, the hawk is coming down, Pinya.' I got to choose the place. I chose a beautiful place I had heard of in the hills and where I'd always wanted to dine but even I knew that a woman no matter how full her purse, did not walk in without a male. I had only driven past it. I offered to help with the bill. We had hardly sat down before Sam began the conversation. It was like someone wanting desperately to use the toilet and just managing to get on the seat before the load comes down.

"It can't work," was what he said. "And it is such a shame, for Espinet was such a good hostess while I was in her country. She protected me; she translated for me; saw that I ate on time and good food. I can do nothing for her here and I am ashamed to say it but I have to tell someone, I can't even stand her body odour which naturally makes intimacy difficult. So there has not been even this basic marriage activity going on. The heat here makes her perspire so much, so that the white person smell is a dozen times enlarged and neither bathing nor perfume will disguise it for long." "What a cheap shot," he added. "I feel like the dirtiest dog for saying something like this about a really fine woman, but I have to say it."

One intimacy deserves another. I told him about Basil and that I hoped he was somewhere thinking and feeling the same frustration with Gerda. I offered that I thought mixed couples should try to find a neutral place.

"Why not try Australia. Both of you will be trying to settle in. That will bring you closer" I said.

"That's hogwash Lily. I am home because I want to be home and this is where I stay."

Sam was like me, a psychologist, so I wasn't surprised when he said. "Call me Basil. Seriously." I did and the venom came down like a lanced boil or the Montserrat volcano erupting. If he had needed help with the cheque, I couldn't do what I had offered to do, for tears were blinding me. We drove down the hill with my tears and moans competing with the engine of the car. Sam took my keys and let me in, found my dressing gown, put me in it and tucked me in bed between my sheets. It was not until morning that I realized that I was in a man's arms and the arms belonged to Sam. He was fully dressed minus his coat and tie. With daylight I realized too that I was lying on his arm rather than in his arms. I am no longer the light weight I was at twenty-one. I had to imagine that in putting me to bed, his arm had fallen under me and to get it out he would have to wake me and he chose not to do this. The man hadn't slept for the night and his poor arm would probably need medical attention. I was impressed. I made him phone Espinet and I spoke to her telling her that I had been ill and Sam had not felt that he could leave me. I thanked her and she said it was decent of me to call her. She thanked me. There was gratitude all around.

Our therapy continued but I told Sam it would have to stop unless Espinet could come in as Gerda. The truth is that physical feelings that I had never experienced with Basil I suppose because I had been so young, were manifesting themselves and I didn't know how to handle them; I didn't want to be alone with Sam. Gerda did come in and I was not alone in my difficulty with controlling my feelings. I could not really handle my feelings for Basil and Gerda, Sam and Espinet nor could Gerda/Espinet handle her feelings towards me. We decided to go formal and get a colleague, a psychiatrist into the play. Lee Grant was game. He was black and had a black wife so his feelings could not be engaged plus he had been looking at the situation on campus and been wondering what could be done about it. Ever the humorist, he added, "We might even get a paper out of this, even a book eh!"

I was sorry for Espinet. Where I could curse the worse Jamaican bad words at Basil/Sam and feel good, she could only one or two times hit Sam's chest with her little albino-looking fists. And we hadn't brought in Sam's girlfriend who seemed to have melted like a snail in salt. Sam told Espinet that they had to face the fact that the marriage was over. He would not release her however until she had signed up for and passed one of those professional courses offered at the University. He suggested social work. With this academic experience and having lived in the multicultural Caribbean she would be well ahead of the game in multicultural Britain and would easily get a job and rise to the top. He apologized. This was not what she had signed up for, he knew, but better could not be done. They had to work with what they had. He would sign his pension over to her. She would never be in want.

Sam and I were the only two black-skinned people seeing each other. Other black-skinned colleagues and nearly all are male, are with brown girls. White men are with very black girls; the white women are either in lesbian relationships with each other, are in voluntary social work or are sitting in the wives' corner in the SCR, lusting after their husbands. No one else seems to feel disturbed enough to seek formal psychotherapy though Lee Grant is willing to help. I think if he ever uses the data it will be in one of those large novels like *The Valley of the Dolls* that women read at the hairdresser under the drier.

Sam and I have the same kind of background, knowing that there is the good life to live at home but never being able to manage it. We attack this missed good life with vim and vigor. There is nowhere worth going that we haven't been. I am making him dashikis – they are so cool and so appropriate in our climate even if they are not top of the style today and in gratitude he is cultivating a beard. We know there can't be a marriage until Espinet has her degree but we are pressing on. I am even willing to start a family. He sees this as feasible. He didn't feel this way with Espinet and we all are glad they weren't fruitful, though if you are to believe them, they were not doing much planting.

I hear that Basil is doing very well. Gerda somehow managed to get him his degree. Sam tells me that part of the beauty of the white wives is that they know how to manipulate the system. Unfortunately they can't do this when they come to your home, for they don't know the system here and don't know the culture. He had me look at the two successful mixed marriages we knew – Roy's and Ken's. Their wives knew every cabinet minister and are permanently on the social pages and give big parties written up in the newspaper: 'Dovecakes, it was time again for Mrs Roy's…to die for end of year party. The professor, Mrs Roy's erudite husband took himself away from his books to serve the most…In attendance were of course the top of the top from cabinet minister to athlete'. He told me of the committees on which these fellows sat by virtue of their wives' work 'socialiting' and how important these committees are to the running of the country. These guys are important indeed.

"You are a native but you can't get to these heights, Lily. Espinet and the other wives either did not know or were not as capable of working the local system as Roy's and Ken's wives." I asked him if it would have made a difference in his marriage.

"Seems like whoring to me and I would have been embarrassed especially as certain other things were not working."

"So I don't have to try to learn from Mrs Roy and Mrs Ken?" I said.

"I am proud enough of the work that you do in this academy and I am proud enough of the work that I do. Going out occasionally to give a little talk is about as much as I can do and I don't need you to find that for me. Moreover, we have a lot of catching up to do with each other. You are still so angry at Basil. I don't know that you have got over him yet. We need to do some more of the things that he didn't do with you so that we have our own history for you to think on. Let Ken and Roy and their wives do what they do best.

The locals I had to try to win were Sam's parents and the wide wide extended family. It was clear to me that they had prized Espinet. Roy's mother was forever saying "What a pity. No children." I think she wanted to see grandchildren with pig tails behind their backs. Yet as she confessed to me, she had wept and wept when she received a photograph with four people in it. The groom, the bride and the two witnesses.

"That was the wedding of my son who had always made me and the whole family proud. His father didn't get to even kill a goat. He sent a letter with the photograph saying that Espinet worked in the library at his university, had been very good to him and had assumed that she was coming back home with him. Had bought summer clothes and given up her apartment and he didn't see how to disappoint her. They had to have a hasty wedding as he knew I would not be able to stand seeing him living with a woman to whom he was not married. And that is true. But still the marriage is not my fault. How everything can get to be the mother's fault so?"

"I was angry with her," his mother continued, "for from what he wrote, it appears that he was not quite ready for marriage and was kind of pushed into it. But when she finally came, she tried so hard to get on with us, I had to love her for that. Could she sweat! She would try to go to the field with Dad or to help me in the kitchen but I would tell her 'No.' I didn't want to see all the liquid leaving her glands and her body desiccated. The climate did not suit her."

Fortunately they knew of my parents and hadn't heard anything bad about us. My mother dragged Sam aside to talk about the dog, Basil. She was as bad as I had been. She even told Sam how I had chopped off my hair because of this misguided boy whom she knew would carry me to perdition. My father said that any man over thirty who is not married is living a slack life. He assumed that Sam and I were living this life. Both of them disliked the slack life that Sam and I were living but as my mother said, from I was seventeen and with that no good Basil, she had told me that my life was mine. Ten years later what can she say but that she hopes it is regularized soon. "That Basil had no pedigree," she told Sam. "We never even heard of his parents." Like Sam's people had of them, they had heard of his people.

"Family of Nemhard from James Hill? Think one of them was inspector of schools round here once," my father remembered. That Sam could say, "That's my uncle," softened the slack life a bit.

Novar is back and it bothers Sam that he and I talk so much. It bothers him that I even have this datum in my head but I think it would be worse to pretend disinterest. Gerda's parents, Novar says, were of the human race so they did not strongly disapprove of the union, and our government was happy to employ him in the diplomatic service. He was sent to Mexico. Good for them. A neutral place. There are no children. I wonder why not, but not in any depth. I am too busy making up for all of that time from twenty-one when he broke off with me to twenty-eight when I met Sam.

My parents don't come to Town to stay over, nor do Sam's so it can't bother them that Sam's books are now in my house and that this is where he works when he is not in the office. He feels he has to take care of Espinet so he is with her for half of the day. That's where his clothes are and where he sleeps most weekdays. She and Beryl, their helper, take care of the house cleaning, and laundry, and Sam and I do grocery shopping. I have no problem with the division of labour especially as the other house is within walking distance. An affair without Espinet's knowledge would have been impossible and very nasty. Thank God that we did this right. I am trying not to ask Espinet too often, how her courses are going.

It was October and as usual there was rain on top of rain. The ground provisions: yam, coco, potatoes and dasheen that were our staple food were water soaked and even smelt rotten when you took them cooked up to your mouth. There were ants in all their glory. They took over. If you put your hand on the window sill, it would be so attacked by ants that you would find a long mark made by bites as if you had had surgery from your wrist to your elbow and the doctor had sewn you up. My father tried to keep them off the dining tables by putting the legs of the tables in the tops of polish tins filled with kerosene oil. The goat kid that our grandmother in her usual style of giving each grandchild something to make his living by, had just arrived for my baby brother. It died. We couldn't play outside for we might catch a cold and die like the goat. The most we could do was read. We must have read everything there was in the house including the minutes of the Diocesan Council and of the All Island Banana Growers meetings.

My mother was not taking this well. She hated the fact that we couldn't go outside and play and that as a consequence there was no peace for her head. She sulked. Thank God the helper had braved the rain and come out, for the other thing my mother hated was having to go into the kitchen in the rain and mud and coax wet wood into flame. When she is this frustrated, my mother's face gets long and her mouth becomes a pig's snout and my father takes this time to tease her: "Ah beg you haul in you mout and gimme likkle pass." My mother was making guava jelly. It made the house smell good but this was an unintended consequence. She was making guava jelly to take her mind off the weather and other things which bother big people. She hated the thought of feeding her family common, ordinary bread. Bread and tea was for poor people who didn't know and couldn't afford to know about nutrition. They had not been part of the food for family fitness programme. But there was nothing else in the shops and nothing in the fields. The guava jelly was to add substance to the bread.

Our house is wood and of course the floor is too. Mother was cooking in a clay pot. I know she was worrying that the coals could fall through the hole at its base and burn the floor. My little brother was in the creeping stage; she was worried that he might get to the pot and turn the boiling liquid on himself. I tried to deal with this worry by keeping my eye on the baby. This meant that I couldn't go up to the pot and watch the liquid turning into waves going in and under each other, watch the bubbles making lace as beautiful as hair pin crotchet. It was a crucial time in the jelly boiling. If it boiled too long now, she would have tied teeth on her hands, jelly that would not spread on bread. She gets a cup of water in which she drops a bit of the boiling liquid. If it forms itself into a sixpence, then the jelly is ready. I couldn't peep and help her to decide for I had to watch the baby. My mother needed all her powers of concentration at this point. I knew I would get the drink, the remains of the testing of the guava jelly in the cup.

We didn't normally lock our doors, especially our back

door for there is always a lot of traffic from the kitchen to the house through that door. But it was closed this time to keep out the rain and the cold. There was a knock on the door at this most inopportune time. My mother's brow knitted with the question: Who could this be? Strangers who need to knock come to the front door. It wasn't Cookie. Dinner was a far way off and she wouldn't knock; she would shout out: "Dinner is ready. I am coming in." or something like that. Who could it be? Mother put her cup and spoon away and opened the door a foot or two. It was an angel.

"Mary," my mother said, "Why are you out in the rain?" Answer. Like the Bavarian girl 'coming from her Deutschland with pretty things laden' and selling brooms, Mary needed to sell 'these garden eggs' in order to get money to buy bread, which garden eggs, the first I had ever seen, she held in crooked arms just like Lady Clare held the 'lily white doe' which her cousin Sir Ronald had just given her. I knew all about these people, for from our community song book, we sang about this Bavarian girl and there was a picture of her at the bottom of the page. Lady Clare and Sir Ronald I learnt about from the many old elementary school texts that my mother collected for our reading on days such as this October one. Though both Lady Clare and the nameless Bavarian girl were village girls, they had on shoes. This angel, obviously related to them, was barefooted and my mother commented to her: "Mary, you are so pale." How silly of my mother. She is pale because she is an angel but Mary kindly answered her: "Where I was, Mam they didn't let me out for me to see the sun and it to shine on me."

"Oh" my mother remembered. "So they had put you away."

"Yes Mam. Because I chop him." She found some money in her change purse nearby and without any bargaining or even setting of price, gave the angel Mary some money and she disappeared from our door, leaving my mother sighing. I had so many questions. For instance, how come an angel spoke so submissively to my mother? It was not my question that framed the communication between me and my mother. She asked as if she was not the best person to know.

"How old are you?"

"Eight, Mam" I answered and then she went on.

"You are not too young to hear this. I hope it never happens to you. You see Mary, there, she was in prison. She was in prison for chopping Andrew. He troubled her and in self-defence she chopped him. How could this be fair?" she wondered to herself. Something told me that the question I was about to ask – "How did Andrew trouble Mary?" would not be answered so I readied myself to listen in to the conversations of Jake and Eulalee our helpers who controlled the kitchen, for my answer.

The story begins:

Mary was the grandchild of the high family that once owned the whole district some long time ago. Jake and Eulalee did not know her parents but something did go wrong. Mary became an orphan, like so many other angels, I thought, and had to be reared by her grandparents. They arranged for a foreign-looking man, they thought, to come and meet Mary and in two two's they were married and repaired to the little house at the gate of the road that leads to the big house. Soon the grandparents died. Mary's husband went off to the war or some such thing, leaving Mary alone in the half furnished house by the gate and a gold ring on her finger. Jake and Eulalee said that Mary must have been cold for the house was so empty. They were sure she was hungry for she never was taught to work, having been served by helpers all of her eighteen years. Moreover, the fellow, whether he knew how to cultivate or not, had not had time to do so, so, Mary Mary quite contrary, had nothing growing in her garden.

People didn't think it odd when they saw Andrew making his way over to Mary's house with breadfruit and all kinds of things, for Andrew, black and with no claims to being part of the heavenly body, had been the yard boy to the grandparents. They even thought it was right that Andrew should be taking things to Mary for no doubt, since Andrew had no land of his own, he was stealing from the standing crops on the old people's abandoned estate – crops which didn't need any constant care and would live even if tied up with withes and other creepers. Of course tiny angelic Mary could not reach them and neither had the strength nor the capacity to chop down a banana or a plantain tree, much less climb a breadfruit tree. Andrew was also finding firewood for her yard and roasting and cooking for himself and Mary whatever he carried in.

People didn't see anything wrong, but while Mary like them, must have thought that Andrew was just extending his yardboy-ship from her grandparents to her, Andrew saw himself as Mary's keeper and started to want wife from her. I was revolted. I had seen cats and dogs and even donkeys giving and taking wife and the thought of Andrew with his black face wrinkled as if it was a black cloth cap stretched from head to chin, with eyes like the monkey I had seen at the zoo in Kingston, his mouth like a black thread bag and his scaly planters on the ground, doing this with Mary, the angel, was unthinkable. Mary should have somebody like Sir Ronald. Not Andrew who didn't even have a pair of tyre sandals to hold the ten tough toes hanging from his planters. Mary's dilemma made me think "What a sin!"

And Andrew liked me. I had in turn liked him. He worked at the butcher's shop and he had made up a name for me. He called me Little Reid, the 'little' made to sound like 'litel'. I did think his naming me thus was something intelligent. He had often heard me playing the recorder and my family name was Reid. After hearing Mary's story, though, the word 'intelligent' was no longer something I linked with Andrew. Dirty was more like it. My mother didn't have to tell me to be wary of Andrew. Now I stopped answering when he called out 'Little Reid' and smiled his crushed cap smile. If I smiled in return, it was because I now knew why he couldn't straighten out his hand. According to Jake and Eulalee, one night after cooking the dinner and eating with Mary, he refused to leave.

"Andrew with him dirty self, for him wasn't a bathing man, and him wood-fire smell want to hold up the lady." Jake said with scorn in his voice. "She promptly went for the cutlass." the story continued. "He must have thought she was carrying it to give it to him as a way of encouraging him to leave," so the storyteller said, "but this was not so." She told him, "I will use this you know if you touch me again." And kept the cutlass. I will always think of Mary holding that cutlass like Paul Bogle holding his at the Morant Bay courthouse in the sculpture done by Mrs Manley. But he didn't believe her and according to Jake he stretched out his hand to caress her. Mimicking Andrew, Jake continues: "He mussi say, 'you pretty you know,' like Mary never know that before. Whoosh go the cutlass on the hand." They said it was a deep cut on the fleshy part of the hand but the bone could be seen. The hand was almost severed and Mary did not make any move to bind it up or anything. She just pushed him out of her little cabin with his bleeding self and went to bed.

Andrew went home leaving a trail of blood behind him and a voice calling "help, help" going before him. Help came and Aunt Leah took over with her herbs and prayers. People said that if there was a hospital around, the doctors could have returned the hand to its normal functioning but no amount of 'nointing' with olive oil could get it to stretch out after Aunt Leah had got it to heal. The DC came for Mary and took her to jail. She had nobody to vindicate for her they said, and that's why they took her to jail and even prisoned her, for some years after, when Carl had troubled Mr Mason's daughter, is him did go to jail, though it wasn't quite the same thing for Delores did not chop Carl. But is true Mary had nobody. They said that if Mary had told the judge that Andrew was trying to get wife from her, he wouldn't have prisoned her, but she was too hoity toity to say things like that and believing some said, that she was Jesus's own sister, she opened not her mouth and was sent to prison.

The judge even cursed her, calling her ungrateful for he had heard that Andrew used to feed her. Nobody told him that he was feeding her with things from her people's place. My angel like St Paul was locked up in prison, which was odd for the angels were not usually imprisoned; they led people out of prison. No angel led Mary out. My mother was one of the few who publicly sided with Mary and kept on doing so, for it is she who first told me that Mary had chopped Andrew in self-defence and seemed to think that this was fair. Andrew belonged to the descendants of slaves in the village and they were many and related by blood. They were vexed with Mary's forebears and therefore vexed with Mary. They insisted that Andrew was only doing her a favour; what Andrew coulda want with a scrawny woman like that; that she had bad blood in her veins passed on from her grandfather and his father and did not know gratitude. Devil must definitely be in her, they said for how a small person like that, can't even cut a cane out of root, can chop a hand so hard that it nearly divide in two. There were even some, Jake and Eulalee told themselves and me eavesdropping, who said, "What if him did even want wife? Wha dat? De husband gaan wey long time and no come back. Ah no nutten for her to give in when de man a look after har so good." And there were those who said, "If she didn't want to give him wife, she shouldn't have did take the food," choosing to forget that the food came from Mary's people's property. And they were vexed.

Mary did not come back with any more garden eggs. I wondered where she had got the first ones for I never saw garden eggs again. I didn't mind too much that she didn't come back with garden eggs for I didn't like the taste at all. I wondered too how and what my angel was eating. It was October and the heavy rains were upon us so that I could not be on the road to see for myself. My last sighting of Mary was therefore my first. We heard that a car had come for her but that she was putting up a fight and didn't want to go in it. That they had just lifted up little Mary with the gold ring on her left hand ring finger and dropped her in the back seat and driven off. Some people said that with the lack of food, for Andrew was not now feeding her, and with the loneliness, Mary, for everyone except perhaps my mother was against her, was off her head and her people had sent the Black Maria for her. Others said is her husband come for her but he away so long Mary didn't recognize him and so was fighting him. Some said it was catcher man come for her but I know this cannot be so for catcher man is black heart man and they want black heart, and angels' hearts are not black. When you see the picture of Jesus with his heart open, that heart look to you like is black? Mary had a white heart so what catcher man would want hers for?

Nobody came to claim Mary's little house at the gate leading up to the big house, nor for that matter, the larger property. People quarreled about the condition of the place. They complained to the MP, that it was a hazard. Bad boys were pulling girls into the bush and raping them there, and from time to time there would be a hullabaloo as someone found a panty or a belt and would bellow on the top of their voice asking to whom these things belonged. They complained about the duct ants' nests and claimed that this was the headquarters of the dangerous pests that could eat down your house in one day. I was fascinated by that and was hoping to see a house being eaten down, for I had learnt in history class that the Spanish had settled at first in St Mary but had had to move because ants were eating all that they had and were producing. I am still waiting.

The reason they saw these ants' nests and the clothes, was that Mary's people's property had now become common land. It was not only Andrew that was cutting bananas and plantains and picking apples and ackee, breadfruit and avocado pear, everybody was eating off this well fruited if badly kept property. And guess what else was there? Horse eye and wild cashew to stone dog and to suit out several games of marbles at recess time. The cashews gave a whoosh sound like thunder when the marbles hit them in the ring. You, the owner felt powerful. The horse eye you could rub until it was hot, and you could then burn somebody with it.

I collected too, but I couldn't let my mother see me going over there for she and I knew that the boys did ask girls to go into the thicket with them and that it wasn't just to collect horse eye and wild cashew. And it wasn't all rape. She didn't want me to see wifing and I didn't want to see it either. In fact that property found its way into a song. The old property owner's name had been Minott, so the place was called Minott. The song was about Jim, short for Jemima, rolling down her drawers at the foot of the breadfruit tree at Minott and finding herself nine months in the way. Even I had been asked to go to Mary's people's abandoned property but of course I hadn't been with any boy. I didn't want to chop anybody and didn't want it said that "mi did well up to it or mi never woulda go," as they said of Jemima. Nor could I forget that most had blamed Mary for not early enough rebuking Andrew.

Pauline

She didn't know what kind of crisis this was. She had heard of midlife crisis but she was too young for that. She had just turned forty. The other one that she knew about was single mother crisis and that she knew very well. Most of the women she knew had gone through that. It came between the ages of eighteen and twenty. She had already been through that: she was forty-one. There was the stopped period and the morning sickness and the fright in the pit of your stomach. This last one was the worse. Followed by telling him and him denying that he had made you pregnant. This is how it was for her and it came with an anger so solid, you needed a knife to cut it.

Fortunately his brothers with whom he shared the house and his neighbours had all seen her at some time leaving his house in the early morning. What could have her there that late? He could barely sign his name so they were not doing homework; she was not teaching him to read and write for everyone knew the position of his father and himself on that matter. Reading and writing was for those NPD people. His party was LSD and the family had not been less off than anybody else for not knowing how to read and write. In fact they were miles better off than some of those jumping up and shouting NPD. So she would not have been fool enough to be there to make him literate nor him sensible enough to be wanting her there to make him literate.

What else could keep her at his house until early morning? He had no DVD or even television that they could be watching late up into morning. So what else could they be doing except that which makes a girl pregnant? Nobody believed his protest and he had been ashamed enough to stop that foolishness when the baby came, for it was the spitting image of his father and everybody said so. This didn't mean that he supported or even liked the child. She had heard that he had said that of his four children there was only one that he liked and the name called was not that of her son. She had managed however, and their son had passed enough subjects in CSEC to get into the police force. And was the boy a beauty! He looked like a nicely scraped roast breadfruit and the women were stretching out their hands to him as if he was indeed yellow heart breadfruit waiting for pear and ackee. All that was behind her now.

She had done well at social studies in high school and later on at college. In fact she had come third in the island in social studies in her CXC year, so she was familiar with the term, 'status' and suspected that her crisis had something to do with that. When she had got pregnant and had begun to show, she knew that she would have to leave college and she did. She had gone there on a scholarship and had just one year left to graduate. The district had been proud of her for getting a scholarship and so was her family for there was no college money waiting in any bureau drawer to be found. Naturally a lot of people were vexed with her and this her action, and its reaction had written her status large – she was a careless, untrustworthy female who make man turn her head. She had lived with this sense of herself and had hardly left her home, but her good friend who perhaps happily had been spared the crisis by a spontaneous abortion, had formed a choir and had asked her to be a member. It was difficult for her to say no for she loved singing.

After the choir took her back into social life, it was church. She was invited into this new aggregation where she met many of her friends who had gone or were going through the first crisis. They had a nice time singing and clapping but she couldn't stand to see the rolled over eyes of the women thrashing on the floor in the spirit. None of her set had got the spirit or wanted to get the spirit, so she supposed none of them would soon be rolling on the floor with someone running to pin up their skirt while their eyes roll over as if they were about to die and they moaned as if they were in the process of making a baby. To hear the elders read from the Bible was sheer torture. She didn't feel comfortable taking her son there and didn't. This was not the place for a child. But what kind of church is not a place for a child?

When Mrs Reid pointed out to her that her family had always been members of her church from way back with great-grandfather and that they needed her singing voice, she had started taking her son there. This was a decent church; there was no rolling on the floor. The people here were very literate. They had to be, for all their prayers and their songs had to be read out of their prayer book and their hymnal. There were under-fourteens in that church, about twelve of them so her son fitted in well. He even got a job he liked. It was carrying the cross from the back door of the church up to the altar. Most of the time there was no organist, for she was one of the school teachers in the elementary school, had recently married and naturally chose to go home some weekends. On these weekends they depended very much on Pauline to raise the hymns and sing loudly.

Under-fourteens there were and over-seventies but there was nobody else in her age group but herself. That was bad enough. On top of this, she began to feel as if she carried the burden of all their hopes. There was Mrs Reid, the church secretary who welcomed everybody by name at every service and always thanked her for her presence and hoped that she would draw nearer soon. It seemed to her that Mrs Reid was expecting her to take over from her at some time. Then there was Mrs McIver. She wore very elegant clothes but didn't seem to do much in the church. Her area was the Citizens' Association and she gave a report on the event had or to be had by this group whenever Mrs Reid asked the congregation as she always did, if there were any notices. Both these ladies gave voice to the opinion that Pauline with her two years of college was just the person to take over the post of secretary for the Citizens' Association, the post being empty since Mrs Curlue got married and had to be in her husband's house so often.

Men. Mrs Reid's husband did come to church but he was so old and short-sighted that she had to lead him in and put him to sit on his special bench. He knew all the responses by heart and all the hymns too but had a habit of coming in late in every song or prayer, so that the production sounded like a round. The children giggled. She thought this was poor Mr Reid's way of getting the group to recognize that he was still a person, Mr Reid's status struggle. The Reids were high: they had a good many cows and acres of vegetables and foodstuff of every kind. Thursday saw all the higglers at their farm gate. Mrs McIver's husband did not come to church but if there was a door to be re-hung or zinc to be replaced, you heard that Mr McIver would see to it. He was really big and high. He too had a farm but along with this he was a contractor, skilled in masonry, woodwork, electricity, everything to do with building. They said he had gone to college to learn this, which was strange, very high, for most carpenters, electrician or masons that anybody knew, simply went to trade with an older one and learnt the trade then started taking in work on his own. In fact Mr McIver had very many boys learning trade with him. The McIvers and the Reids were the upper class. If a stranger came into the village, he was likely to stop at their house to greet them before going on his way. Even district people's children who had gone out and done well, felt that had they to stop at their houses and greet them before they came to their own parents.

Between them they controlled their church; they controlled the Citizens' Association and the JAS and any other groups with external connections. It would not be odd for the four of them to decide that although there was an agricultural society there, they needed to establish a group to see about coffee and they could be heard discussing away at a coffee meeting as if they had not met the day before in the Citizens' Association or the JAS. They went to half yearly meetings of the JAS; they went to annual meetings and you could see them making a point at a televised meeting. They were so much in the front line that people outside thought that a lot was going on in their village. They seemed to be quite happy to have meetings with just the four of them.

Pauline knew of nobody else that they were inviting to their meetings except her. Occasionally she accepted an invitation. She had gone to synod with the three of them – the two ladies and Mr Reid. She understood nothing. She didn't know whether they understood either. They couldn't answer her questions but they were ever so happy to be there and happy that she was there that the question did not get justice. It didn't seem to bother them that they didn't understand what was being said and read. She was not happy to be there. That was bad enough but worse was the feeling she had that those hands with their engagement rings and married rings, hands which had shaken those of so many important people were wanting to imprison her in foolishness. She could see herself in a large garbage dump into which these ladies, each holding one of her hands had swung her like a waste-paper basket into this pit of words on old envelopes, on typed paper too crushed for her to read, papers shredded that she would have to put together again if she was to be able to read and understand what the message was.

She felt so lonely at the edge of the pit with them. And lonely in the pit with those words that apparently didn't want to be deciphered. It was a dilemma. She liked words. This was the upper class into which she was being invited but her body kept crying out that she could not be the future of the church, of the Citizens' Association and of the JAS and anything else they chose to form. What a weight to be the one inheritor and this inheritor could not understand what those meetings were for. Why did the minutes have to be confirmed and why did their church confirm people and not baptize them as so many others did? And was it the same 'confirm'?

With her son in the police force, and getting good money, she was a free woman, she could do what she wished and she wished to further her studies, to take up what she had left to have and raise her son. She hadn't told them anything about it. She had gone to Bay and registered in a programme there. By the next day, passing Mrs Reid's house, she felt like she had done the wrong thing for there was Mrs Reid congratulating her for making the move. As a matter of fact she already knew of a situation she could fill as soon as she had her certificate. She had to smile thanks but she also had to wonder if they were tar baby and she was Nanny Goat and the lesser animals stuck to tar baby and getting more stuck as you struggled to get out of their range.

She got her certificate. The offer Mrs Reid had held out did not materialize. She was glad for she didn't know if she would have had the strength to refuse it. Good social scientist that she was, Pauline soon learnt that the upper crust ladies bothered her because she had credited them with importance. And what had they really done? Got someone to marry them. She would dig herself out of their pit of indecipherable words. She would arrange her life so that they wouldn't want to invite her to have drinks with the minister where she was wont to be paraded as the 'up and coming', the evidence that the church was still alive, or introduced to the MP to show that the new government policy was holding firm for here was one who had fallen by the wayside and was now taking advantage of the lifelong learning programme to get herself back on stream. Pauline thought hard. It was true that her great-grandparents had been a part of the church to which the Reids and the MacIvers went but they had also been higglers both, not having a square of land on which to plant anything while they had so much. She was that too; she would revert to being be a higgler.

She had gone to Mr Reid like everybody else to trust her first load. He was on his wide verandah. When her turn came to speak to him, he just said "Sit down" and pointed her to one of the slat chairs. She had to wait until the sun was up in the sky before he turned to her. She was not surprised at this action for she had been expecting something out of the ordinary but not from him. He said, forcing his weak eyes to look into hers: "Your dress and your apron so new even the place where they fold the cloth in the store is still evident to me a blind man. You think this is Louise Bennett recitation you dress up for? Anyhow you know that you going to succeed for you always succeed. You make for success. But let me tell you that that is your problem. Not those two old women who have to do the same thing every day to feel that they are alive. Where you going after this higgler business? You going set up shop? You can jump from one thing to the other and still succeed. Mi sorry fi you. Gwaan gal, mek them give you what you want and bring mi mi money next week."

It was hard but it was exciting. To begin with, she had to cook for the school from Monday to Thursday, rush Thursday evening to look her load and get up by four o'clock Friday morning to catch Mass Derven going to Porus market. The man would have them up waiting from four and sometimes don't come until six o'clock. By the time they reach Porus is nearly midday and their regular customers buy from somebody else. Sometimes he don't come at all and they are left with the load to rot on their hands though they still have to pay for it. Somebody had to speak to him and they pushed her forward for after all she had subjects and he respected her. What here too! Of course she spoke to Mass Derven and there was change. Now if they had a problem with the market attendant, it was she, though she hardly knew the market runnings. Didn't even carry any lime to bless her spot and had to carry scale for she just hadn't learnt yet to weigh with her hands.

One time after that she went to order and collect her load up at Mr Reid and as he hear her voice he give out a Keekee laugh. "What mi tell you, Miss Success. Mi hear sey you all turn union delegate! Bet you ready to run from higglering now. You just don't want the responsibility that you train yourself for. You want freedom. Want breeze to blow right round you. You don't want no responsibility. Girls like you cuss the baby father bout how him irresponsible but if he want you to marry and make life with him, Oh No Sir. Ah tie him want tie mi down. If angel Gabriel or even Selassie who oonoo sey oonoo love, ride him white horse come here and with his sword at his side, bow down on one knee and ask you to marry him, the same said answer he would get: Ah tie you want come tie mi down. Ah Mrs Reid mek me. And any man you see bout the place can put two coins together, look out and see if a nuh some woman strengthen him so him can mek it. Even eena the government business and any church, nuh have fi look too hard fi see how the women dem a hold the thing up. You might nuh see them face everyday eena *Gleaner*, but ah them. Ah dem a di leader. Ah dat gift you have. Mrs Reid dem didn't know how to lead it out of you but somebody else will. Mark my words."

Tansey's choir needed gowns but who had more than the money to send the children out to school? She had convinced the group that a little buying and selling could get them enough money to buy these uniforms. The seven of them subsequently joined themselves into a market cooperative. They had meetings where she found herself telling them about minutes and the need to keep minutes – "they are a record. None of us head can remember everything that was said every week and we need to know what we had said if we are to go on with planning, so it is best to have minutes. And 'confirm'? Well nobody is an angel and we can write down the wrong thing. Confirm means that what write down is what really was said, for all of us remember it that way and we confirm that is so it did go." While she was talking she was hearing Mrs Reid and Mrs McIver and she wondered if all people with ambition came to those forms and those roles. She hoped she wasn't pulling people to her and turning up their blouse sleeves which were not intended to be turned up or straightening a collar which didn't need any straightening as those old women were given to doing. She couldn't stand it. This need they had to touch people, certainly to touch her. She hoped she didn't have that need.

Mr Reid needed his joke. Everywhere he saw her he was calling out to her as the president of the higgler association and telling people how proud he was of her. What a set of fools were the men these days. In his time a woman like she would have six men following her for they knew the value of women then. Would it ever stop? This adulation. No. It was time to accept it. She had leadership qualities. She could choose whatever group she wished to lead. She was leader of the higglers. At least she was leader of something and of people whom she understood. Could even take over from Mrs Reid and Mrs McIver if she wished.

She wondered if that cockroach had heard Mr Reid

talking about her in glowing terms and saying that men were foolish for not having chosen her to lead them. He had the nerve to tell her that if he ever decided to get married, she was the one baby mother that he would want to marry. "Mi would mek you lead me, you know." Who was that dirty foot cloth talking to? When she did not reply he continued on another track. "So wi son get promotion. Big man into traffic department. Then Pauline, you mean you couldn't send the boy sometimes come spend time with me so mi coulda know him good and him coulda know mi. Mi hardly know what him look like and mi nuh know if mi see him since him eleven for pickney like dem de a school all the time, you hardly can see them. Mi drive truck. If him fi bring up him own father, him should ah know ah who him a bring up. Him could a do it fi spite, but him must know sey a spite him a do it for. Suppose mi go pass a money to a police and find out sey a mi own son mi ah ask fi let me off, nuh worse than embarrassment fi mi and him?"

This was the longest conversation they had had about their child. She couldn't help it, she had to answer. "Mi know anything bout you and your son? Me don't even know how much you have." She was a bit surprised to hear him say: "Mi no have no more than mi did have when you tell me sey you a mek baby fi mi. Mi did stop fool round after Basil born you know."

"Try you bes'," was all she said in the new slang of dismissal. He didn't stop bothering her, and friends were teasing her: "Old time sinting come back again and old fire stick easy fi ketch up." It was time for her to make some things clear.

"The time is well past when I could deal with an illiterate

man," she had said in a public place and someone had retorted: "Hi man! Is your baby father you know."

"Well do I know" she had replied, "And I hope my son doesn't suffer for having a father who could only get a driver's licence because he could buy it. That father couldn't spell out the letter on a stop sign, if you paid him." This conversation took her to the understanding that she was talking about social mobility and acknowledging that she was making a comment on her own mobility.

With the reappearance of the baby father had come a reconnection with the two old ladies. She wasn't lonely now. She had Mr Reid to tease her; she had the choir of which she was now the manager and she had her group of higglers of which she was the president. It was she who went to Mrs Reid and said that she would return to sing for them whenever they wanted her to. Just call. She figured that if Mr McIver could be so much a part of the church without actually coming to church so could she. Like him she would be a consultant to the church.

She had also told her group that the two old ladies had something to offer them: they did craft work very well. Hair pin crochet, tatting all sorts of things that they could learn from them. They wanted to help and the way to handle their help was to tell them what you wanted of them. Otherwise they would smother you with what they thought you should know and you would be choking in their kindness. Mrs McIver and Mrs Reid were invited to one session of the meeting of the higglers and helped to cut the gowns for the choir. In return, the choir gave them two items at their harvest service. Pauline herself went to their church whenever she felt like it and was now able to handle the effusive welcome. She was quite pleased with the nature of her relationship with these people. Her crisis was now over; she had passed 'social control'. You can be quite comfortable in social relations if you know where and how to draw the line between self and others. This is a skill you must have if you are migrating to a higher social status. And the migration should take place but it had to be on your terms.

renville Town is a district so small that it is not even mentioned on the road maps, and its name has not been painted on any finger posts, so that while the Registrar of Births and Deaths would not hesitate to say that Zackie Grenville hailed from Epsom, St Mary, he knew better than that, he was from Grenville Town.

When you turn off the main road, you have to walk along the white gravel road until you hear the Sam River. Just round the corner, you will see the Lee Bridge and you will know that you are on the right track. You are in Epsom proper. Now, if you turn left into the path leading up the hill, you will see a heap of stones under a guango tree, two or three thatched cottages on both sides of the path and then a quarter finished stone nog house. You have reached Grenville Town. This is where Zackie Grenville has lived for as long as he can remember and this is the house that Grandfather Grenville left Zackie to finish.

No one really knows the story of Grenville Town but the older people say that Grandfather Grenville's grandfather had been a slave driver in the long ago days and that when Missis Queen gave the free papers, he settled on that spot. They could be right. If you examine the stone steps leading from the water hole to the Church, you too would think that this place had something to do with those long time days. Folks say that the steps led to the slavery days store house and they still talk about the days when the white

Missis used to carry her horse to the water hole and meet her overseer lover there. But nobody really knows.

There are many other towns around like this. Reid Town, Walker Town, to mention a few, where everybody is related by blood and share more or less the same surnames, where all the faces have a mahogany complexion, favouring direct African descent and where there are stories of an ex-slave founder. So Grenville Town is not unique and if you read the history of the country, you will see that the folk stories might even be true. Zackie's great-great-grandfather might well have been a slave driver as Zackie thought. If he was, then Zackie inherited his bearing from him; if he wasn't, then faith in the truth of this story gave him a kind of confidence and a feeling of superiority.

Actually this feeling of confidence and superiority used to bother Zackie. He knew that he had done nothing to feel superior about, for while his cousins had modernized their inheritance and had turned to banana and cocoa cultivation and had become big fellows talking with ministry officers and going to farmers' meetings, he was then struggling with the sugar cane on a soil so tired he couldn't get enough to see his way to finishing the house and feared that he would as a result, never feel secure enough to belong to the set who preached from the pulpit of the Anglican church on demboy Sundays or who attended half-yearly meetings of the AIBGA or the JAS. In those days he knew these things mattered to him and he couldn't quite make up his mind whether he was to grudge the cousins or to try to follow their fashion. Yes, that feeling of superiority and confidence had been a strong thing but there had been strong now and again doubts about the justness of the feelings.

He was glad now that he had met Rosa for she had

made him give up the foolish struggle to catch up with the cousins and had brought him the joy of a one eye man in a blind eye man's country. He remembered the day she had brought the message to him. "Zackie, I get a dream bout you," she had said, coming round the kitchen where he had been sharpening his cutlass, wondering when he would find a way to put a decent covering upon even one of the rooms of the dead-lef. It was a hard time but even if he had not been in malice with the cousins over the four stone nog walls that Pappy, their common grandfather had left him, he wouldn't be asking them for even a penny loan. Not even the use of their names to get a loan at the PC bank much less selling them a gill of his labour. There would have to be some other way.

He had known Rosa for a long time. He knew she was a good quadrille partner and always in demand. He remembered those days of Sunday school cantata when he was really proud to sing a duet with her, for she could even from those days, sing well. He heard that she could crochet the fluffy ruffles that opened like roses; he had bought slices of her cake at fairs and he knew that she had a hand in the cooked lunches which her aunt and adopted mother, Miss Jen, prepared for him; knew that she helped Miss Jen with the higgler business and knew that he needed someone like Rosa, but something kept him from thinking of her too seriously. She was not from the top bracket: not secretary of the community council, Sunday school teacher in the Anglican Church or any such thing. Nobody the cousins would marry. He was however pleased that she dreamt about him. That was nice and it was a long time since anything nice had happened to him. Yes. He missed the old man. Miserable and all that but he was the only parent he knew and well, in spite of everything, it was nice now that he looked back, to be as necessary to someone as he had been to his grandfather in the last days. Let them malice him. He had a right to that dead-lef.

"Yes. Your grandfather dream me," she was saying to him above the sound of his file against his cutlass. "Right near morning too so I know that what he tell me have to happen. He wake me and ah feel me head grow big and he say, 'I am a old man and I won't trouble you. I just want you to know that you must take care of Zackie'. I know is him but still I wake Aunt Jen and I describe him to her and she agree that is him alright." Without even waiting to see whether he had been attending to what she was saying, she continued, "Zackie I staying."

He didn't know what to answer so he said nothing, but he thought that after all Rosa wasn't that far beneath him. Rumor had it that her real father was someone high up in politics. He hadn't answered her. He went to move his cow as he usually did at that time of the morning and came back to find the house tidy, Rosa's grip in a corner and young smoke coming from the kitchen. Whether she stayed or not would prove a momentous step for Zackie and he knew it. It would decide whether he belonged to the rest of his name or at the bottom with people like Miss Jen. There really was no problem for Rosa for everybody thought that she ought to have moved in with some decent man ages ago.

It was a housekeeper–master relationship for longer than those people seeing her moving in with her grip would think. Thinking back, Zackie did not know what to call the thing that had existed between them. It had a name though. It wasn't the sort of thing that the children read to him from the books which they were now so busily borrowing from the bookmobile. Rosa wasn't in that. It was more like what St Paul talked about but it was even better than that. He didn't know the name but he would find it someday. He knew though that during those early days she had impressed him with her patience. She was Job. He did all he could to discourage her but she won the cold war. She was an angel in disguise and like them, as invisible when necessary.

Only those who saw Rosa walking to his place with her grip, and he supposed Miss Jen, could know that she was there. It was not like Rosa to be sitting out in the yard combing her hair or anything like that and neither he nor anybody else could say that they saw her small clothes on the blue bell tree on which she spread the washed clothes to dry. The most any stranger would hear was a little humming and she could turn that off as tight as a new tin of polish if she suspected that the feet coming were ones that were coming to faas in Zackie's business.

There was nothing Rosa couldn't do. Chicken, cabbage, orange grew like token, for one of the first things Rosa taught him was that a small man had to plant in a small way. Planting like he had, acres of banana and cane could not be his way. He had to use every square inch of his plot both beneath and above so that yam under chocolate under banana, under coconut beside mahoe trees would have to be his way, couple little chickens and some rabbit dropping to manure the place would have to be his way. And every one of those crops could be sold for immediate money except the mahoe tree which would have to stay and mature to turn into lumber to make beds and other furniture. A small way for a small man with a small plot, she used to say. See, he had taken her advice and knew now that behind all that facade, the cousins were wishing that they had followed him and diversified. Them following him! What a blessed thought.

He had immense respect for that simple straightforward woman who managed to give him every fibre of her existence without making him feel guilty; who had been wise without letting him feel foolish; who could seem to give in yet have her way. He could go on like this but all would amount to the greatness of Rosa. She had not given him a child of his own but Delacita whom she reared was so sweet that in spite of his first objections he had willingly let her mind her as their own, carrying his name. After all they were neither of them doing anything that had not been done for them. Neither of them could claim to know their real parents. His had left him with his grandfather and gone off to Colón no more to be heard of; her mother had gone off to work in Town and brought her back to her sister. So it seemed the cycle would go on.

So he had married Rosa but in spite of this or because of this – he still didn't know which – did not go back to the Anglican Church. The Lord had sent Pastor Reid to them and through him he had really turned his back on the church of his cousins. He had found the Lord and it was good. Take for instance tithing. It was a funny thing: you put your hand deep in your pocket and give to the Church the last money you have, then your property start to give you one hundredfold like the Bible said it would – every fowl start to lay and every cow call for bull and you have to ask the condensery to send you two milk pails instead of the one.

It was good to look at that stone nog house and to know

that it was chiefly through your efforts that it now had three rooms complete with roof and ceiling; it was good to preach at church on Sundays; good to have your fellow members next to you for encouragement and advice; good to listen to your voice raising a hymn; good to be decent, upright, honest with yourself and respected by your neighbours. And best of all, good to know that on the rare occasions on which you met the cousins you were no longer the one who had fallen by the wayside, but the one-whose-ways-are-different-from-yours-but-equal-ways. It was more than good to give them a day's work without feeling like the yard boy.

Rosa had done it all. She didn't wear fancy heels or straighten her hair. Even when times were good, she wore her coarse boots made right there in Grenville by Slam. "This is real leather" she would say, "and the boot is constructed to fit my feet. Nobody has me in mind when they building those shoes that anybody can buy and moreover is plastic and that just dry out your skin." So Rosa's yard shoes, shined 'til you could see your face in it, were also her going out shoes. Her hair she wore in plaits with a horseshoe nail as a pin. And Rosa was the lady with the straightest back and the neatest look wherever she and her shoes and her horseshoe nail turned up.

Whenever he dreamt of heaven he saw Rosa there. If she didn't reach no one would. That woman must really have had a special pact with God. Even her end was her design. He could see that night well. Dusk and the telegram telling him to come for the body, the truck and the singing and everybody being kind – Sunday best behaviour. That truck took four hours to get from Linstead hospital to Lee Bridge. Of course the road was not yet asphalted. He had wondered all the way back if he had done the right thing. Rosa had always said she didn't want to die in any hospital and she didn't want to go, but how was he to keep her at home when there was a chance that the doctors could help her? But that woman wouldn't rest 'til she got what she wanted – to blow her last breath in her own house. Zackie heard it and all Grenville Town can testify to it. Rosa sighed as they lifted her supposedly dead body on to the bed. He didn't know how it happened and he didn't want to know. He only knew that Rosa had said she wanted to blow her last breath in her house 'mongst her husband and child and her friends and contrary to all indications, she did.

Today at seventy – three score years and ten as the Bible calls it – Zackie saw himself with grandchildren at secondary school doing well, all amply supplied by Delacita whom no one could get to believe that she was not his own blood; saw his blood children holding their own in the civil service. Mark you, he was not altogether pleased, for he had hoped that some one of them would stay on the land: the Grenville soul was mixed with it and to leave it was to exist as shell but he supposed this was progress and who was he to spell out progress to anybody under seventy. Give thanks, there would be no problem with the name. Two sons and four grandsons, Zackie Granville would live on. Even that Rosa had seen to.

It was she who had sent him to Nita. She had visited him in a clear dream, clear like he had never had and didn't expect that he would ever have again. He had taken the early morning bus to Bog Walk and seen her sitting at the shop piazza, stale drunk, leaning her head on the closed door and looking up, just as Rosa had said she would. He had had to fight with her and for her but he was pleased that he could give her the spiritual aid that Rosa had given him. He had watched Nita heal under his care and she had certainly been a credit to him.

Life had not been without its ups and downs but it had been good. How many men had a good woman in their life. He had experienced two. What else could a man ask for?

I am now thirty-five years old and have six children three of whom are girls. One is fifteen, my age at my first pregnancy. I can't imagine my 15-year-old pregnant. How did it happen to me? My boss who has studied Jamaican women say that we see pregnancy like a bucket of water perched precariously on a ledge under which we must pass and we simply expect the bucket of water to fall on us, that means that we expect to be pregnant whether we want to or not and do precious little to avoid it. I don't know what my teenage daughter is doing but I surely would be surprised if she let that bucket of water fall on her. My boss says I owe it to myself and my daughters to try to understand how the bucket came to fall on me. It is not something I like to think about but if I have to, I have to.

At the time I got pregnant I was going to high school. My mother still declares that I am the brightest of her many children. I don't know if this is so but my teachers did say I had a good head and even today my boss's friends are always being amazed at my choice of language and I have no difficulty in handling the minutes as secretary to the two organizations that I have joined – the parent teachers' association and my political party group. I mention this because I know that my peers are always shying away from any task which requires them to read and write. Not so with me. How does a bright 15-year-old high school girl with an interest in her lessons get pregnant for an old Indian man whose speech is indistinct, who cleans his throat every morning so loudly that virtually the whole village can hear, that like the rooster we did not own, awoke us in our home every morning, and who is the laughing stock of the village?

To begin with, my mother and my several brothers and sisters and I and her occasional lovers shared a house with this man. I never saw my mother in any actual baby-making event but I did know that she had to be, for she was often pregnant. In time I was able to associate certain noises with baby-making. I can't recall ever wanting to make these sounds or make a baby. Children at school did talk about pregnancy and how people got pregnant. Our lifestyle and guidance counselling classes were now talking about those things but most of us were bored by this talk of fallopian tubes and preferred to listen to the whispering of our peers. I can't even say that I relished this whispering for I felt that they were whispering about my mother. Boys shouting out what they wanted to do to you and trying to touch you appealed more to me. Perhaps we felt that we should do to ourselves first what the boys were swearing they would do to us and some of my friends were using all sorts of implements to do these things to themselves. It was about this time when my mother had done what she did and was beginning the making of our seventh sibling that I heard a discussion this man was having with my mother about the sexuality of girls and which had me thinking about myself as a female person.

They were talking about a girl whose parents were trying to separate her from a boyfriend of whom they disapproved. But this girl would jump though the window and run off to this fellow's home. There was nothing her parents could do to keep her away from this man. Mr Manichsingh, my odd neighbour was saying to my mother that as long as a girl is over nine years old, she must have sex and will break any bonds to get it. I was ten then and I remember wondering whether that girl could ever be me. And my answer was 'no, I didn't think so'. I certainly didn't want to be so much in the power of any boy or man that I would be jumping through any window to get to him. Could this be why I began to join the group that did these things to themselves?

It was about this time also that Mr Manichsingh started exposing himself to me. I call him 'Mr' only because I am writing this. From I know myself, how you are addressed has been a measure of respectability in our village. If your right name is John Brown, you will be called 'John' as a child. When you become a respectable adult, you will either be Mass John or Mr Brown. I grew up as Suzzette. None but my close friends or my mother and her close friends dare call me Suzzette now that I am over thirty years old, the mother of big children and a married woman. I am now either Miss Suzzette or Mrs Walker. My neighbour never graduated to Mass or Mr Nobody, not even my youngest brother crawling on the floor called him anything but 'Manichsingh' or any version of this sound that gave utterance when addressing him or talking about him. He was not considered respectable and more than that he was a very nasty man. Instead of using the board latrine that came with the house, he preferred to dig a hole in the bush and do his business there. We had to walk through this bush to get to the public standpipe. I would often catch Mr Manichsingh at his toilet business and it was easy to see his private parts but lately he had been waylaying me and pushing out his penis and doing all sorts of things he must have thought were wonders, with it. He was very proud of it. I cannot say whether the pride was transferable but I began to be fascinated by the show Manichsingh was putting on. It certainly gave me a better idea of how to design that which I was using. He knew I was fascinated and was now pretending to be vexed saying, "All the time mi ah show you and you nah show me nutten." He never did get me to show him anything though he continued to show me and whoever would look.

By the time I was fourteen then, and in formal biology classes, I knew Mr Manichsingh's private parts very well. Some things that school lesson didn't tell me and wasn't interested in telling me, this man's graphic lessons did. For instance, he told me, "Is not the whole of it have to go up into you, so you don't have to fraid to use it." His comment did make 'it' seem more friendly and less frightening. The size of these things had always discouraged me from any personal interest in the real ones. Men in our village are not shy of pulling their zip or buttons and taking a long pee anywhere. So I had seen a variety of these and been horrified at the size of some. It is perhaps this word and the accompanying displays from Mr Manichsingh that made me less cautious and more adventurous. In any case many of my group were becoming sexually active with males and telling us that it didn't have to hurt for like Mr Manichsingh had said 'is not all of it have to go up into you.' And they added you didn't have to get pregnant for they had done it and were not pregnant. I tried it with the fellow whose family owned the biggest store in the town near to us, and I didn't feel any pain. It certainly was more pleasant than that which I had been using. Why did I go into the toilet at school and do this with that boy? Why? I suppose it was just something to try, like a new crochet pattern or a new game or like boys try ganja, a rite of passage. This boy and I were not even boyfriend and girlfriend, though after the toilet thing he would see to it that I got some of the bubble gum which he stole from his parents' shop.

I suppose it was just a stone's throw from letting that fellow go into me in the school toilet to not pushing Mr Manichsingh out of ours. He must have been watching and peeping at me in the toilet for he chose a good time. I was doing what I wouldn't have liked anyone to see me doing, when the door slowly opened and I heard, "Cho Susie you coulda did call me," in a voice that sounded as if it was chastising me. I had no chance to answer for he took out of my hand that which I was using, lifted me from the latrine seat and pulled me onto his private parts. I can still hear that goat voice saying as if he and I had planned something: "Mi nah stay long you know, just a touch and go for this no private. Another time we can go more." I was ashamed that he could think of me as his collaborator and knew no matter what he had said about nine-year-old girls, this teenager would not be with him another time and certainly would not be jumping through any windows to get to him. He really didn't stay long, I must say that for him. Very shortly after he lifted me up, he was backing out of the toilet. But I got pregnant and I know it was through him for the boy at school now had a girlfriend and did not seek me out. Nobody had touched me there with his tool in a long time except Mr Manichsingh.

What to do? I was good at athletics mainly track. I was now turning out for hurdles and high jump in the hope that I would strain myself or fall and abort. I now carried two buckets of water in the wash pan on my head in the same hope, that I would strain myself when lifting that load. When cleaning our rooms, I would crawl under the bed and use my back to lift the iron frame on which the mattress sits, sometimes with the children on it. They took it for a joke: I was giving them a ride. For me it was my way to an abortion. I tried eating young june plums, even donkey's turd and regularly drank a tea of pennyroyal leaves. I did anything that I heard of. Nothing worked. My mother herself was spitting and vomiting to the delight of her current boyfriend. I watched her symptoms. I didn't have to watch too hard for she had been that way often: I could remember. Anyhow, any feelings of nausea like she was exhibiting, that came to me, I quickly swallowed. It was the style of the girls at school to wear the belt to the uniform as a necklace. That suited me well for my belly was getting big. And my belt could no longer hook. Mr Manichsingh knew my condition. He had seen me collecting pennyroyal. That nasty man told me that to prevent my mother from finding out, I should give him one of the towels I used 'at that time of the month', and he would arrange to put some blood on it and if ever my mother accused me of being pregnant, I should show her that blooded towel. My poor mother is largely pregnant when somebody tells her that I might be. Not as bright or as venal as Mr Manichsingh, she asks for evidence and I duly advance the blooded towel that Mr Manichsingh has contrived. She is quieted.

Meanwhile he advises me that we have to see the doctor. "Who? Me and You? I not going anywhere with you," I tell him. Very sensibly he tells me: "Having a baby is not easy and you could dead. You have to go to doctor and nurse so that dem can give you medicine and tablet." He says he has some money and he will pay for everything if we have to pay but he thinks it is free at the clinic.

"But how we going go out there?" I ask him. He tells me that we don't have to go together. He would take the bus two houses down the road and I would take it at my house just like I do when I am going to school. The clinic was on my way to school so after I was seen by the doctor I could easily find a route taxi and just go on to school without anybody being the wiser. This worked. Me coming into the bus, not even turning my head when he comes in but knowing that he is there. We don't even talk or brush against each other as we go into the clinic and he doesn't come forward when the nurses are attending to me, to say anything. One nurse actually did say, though: "Are you here with this girl Sir?" His answer was of course, "No."

We found a place where he could put money and I could go and pick it up. Where on earth did he get money? He was old and stumbled a little and with this had somehow managed to get himself on the pauper roll. It was also said that he was good at gambling. By whatever way he got, Mr Manichsingh would leave a twenty dollar bill for me ever so often. This I put in my Bible. I didn't even know what I was saving for. The people my mother used to work for, let her have the pick of worn clothes. One bundle had along with the usual old clothes, an elasticized panty. This I used to disguise the size of my belly. One day I had to go to work for my mother she being too heavily pregnant to work. The lady asked me, "How your belly look so square?"

"How you mean Mam?" I responded, but she couldn't tell me what she meant. She is the only one who noticed any difference in me. I suppose everybody including her had their own problems to deal with and couldn't be bothered with guessing why a 15-year-old girl was looking so square. After that I started walking sideways in the hope that nobody would see my whole profile and my squareness.

I have to admit that I was relieved when the baby came. I was tired of the deception, of dealing with Mr Manichsingh as if he and I were in some kind of plot together. My mother had just come from her last appointment with the clinic before going to the hospital to have her baby. She had kicked off her shoes and was lying on the bed in her going out clothes. I felt a searing pain and could not straighten up. On all fours I crept to where she was lying down. I had on no panty. I had stopped bothering with those for all the elastics of mine had already gone slack. I now wore the elasticized panty my neighbour had left in the bundle. I slit the seat so that it could go easily up to my waist and I used a bit of raw cloth from the same bundle to hold it in place around my belly. As I was creeping to my mother, I was aware of water following me like I was weeing but I wasn't. By the time I reached my mother, I heard her say, "Suzzette you ah have baby. See it there a pull pon the ground follow you." She turned me and the trailing baby over with her toe, and not even bothering to disinfect her sissors as I know she should, she reached for it and cut the baby from me. She never quarelled. She just said amazingly quietly: "Suzzette you nearly make mi lose my friends. Dem sey you pregnant and mi sey a jealous dem jealous you for you ah do good a school and if anything eena you belly a them get obeah man fi put frog een deh. Mi have fi go tell them now sey dem did right and beg them pardon."

Then she asked the question I feared: "A foo fah?" I did not answer. The question and the non-answer were not unusual as there were traditionally less straightforward but just as effective ways of getting the answer. Rumors normally abound and the fingered guy and/or his mother usually turn up to look at the baby and say whether it is his. I know of a case where a disreputable old man turned up and the girl's mother chased him from the yard. He was not really the father nor had he even had sex with the girl. He was just looking to upgrade his status. It makes men feel big to have produced a child, so they will come and lay claim even if they can't or don't intend to support the child. The girl never said a word but the real father turned up several years later and seeing that his face was stamped on the child, asked the mother if he could be the father and she said yes. This was when the child was about three years old. He has been supporting the child ever since. There was no problem in my not answering. It was more or less expected given that there was no observable boyfriend, but I couldn't afford to let the father-naming follow this traditional course. My problem therefore was how to keep Mr Manichsingh from coming to make a claim.

My mother's door is rarely closed but when it is, everyone knows that she is definitely not available. It was usually only closed when her lover is here. She closed it now and gave me my first lessons in obstetrics and gynaecology. Her movements were restricted by her size so she couldn't show me; she told me what to do, how to deal with the after birth and to suckle the baby. While these lessons were going on, we heard a knock on the door. This must be a great emergency if that was one of the family – one of the children must have cut himself or somebody got burnt and needed to be taken to the hospital. It was Mr Manichsingh. My mother opened the door a few inches and asked what was so important that he had to come calling.

"Mi hear like somebody bawling so mi come see if anything wrong with Suzzette or you or any of the pickney dem." For his effort he got: "Manichsingh, tek youself from me door, you and you goat voice. Just come fi peep fi go carry mi business go a road. Nothing no wrong wid nobody. Gwan bout you business." She made the sound of a goat and muttered, "Damn unsingh" Fine. Manichsingh was dismissed. As I go over these events, I can understand and be amused by what he must have been feeling. Manichsingh was the lowest of the low in that village. He knew everybody's business and talked about it. Nobody talked about his for it was felt that he had none. Now, here was Mr Manichsingh having business that would make good gossiping and discussion but he was not allowed to claim it. I was left in the room while my Mother went to do her usual chores. I heard her telling the children not to let Manichsingh back in our part of the house. She was trying to stop the rumour mill but I needed to stop more than that. I needed to do something to stall Mr Manichsingh if not stop him forever. I tried a long shot. There was Ivan, the boy in the toilet. I sent for him. Fortunately by now my mother had 'taken in' and gone off to the hospital.

No matter how black-skinned we are, most of us have some Chinese or Indian or white blood in us and our baby need not take our colour. My baby was yellowish and I was jet black. This fellow was black-black too. He was pleased to have his name called on this non-black baby. You should see his face light up when he saw the baby! Though he was so black, he had produced a brown baby. It was like not studying but passing an exam. He told his parents of his new status and baby food and clothes came.

Meanwhile two things happened. My mother on leaving for the hospital asked her sisters to keep an eye on us as I was not 'hard enough' after the baby to take charge. So my aunts now knew that I had lied and lied and was now a mother. Mr Manichsingh took advantage of my mother's absence to come knocking on the closed door. I would not let him in. Knowing how I had lied, my aunts were willing to give him a hearing when he complained to them that the baby was his and I would not even allow him to see it. He related all the subterfuges that we had established to support my denials of pregnancy. He told them to look in the Bible and see how much money he had given me. The Bible gave evidence: there were about six twenty dollar bills there. Who was giving me money? They looked at him and at the baby and came to the conclusion that it was more likely to be his than Ivan's. It really was the dead stamp of him. I gave in and admitted it to be his. My whole story now belonged to the village. Of course it reached Ivan's ears. He even came and took back what things had not been opened.

Fortunately I had a lot to learn about mothering and so I had little time for shame. My mother came back with her baby. She had very little time to deal with the village, no time for denials, vexations, for the village radio. We just took life as it came. I faced the next step head on. Mr Manichsingh was to have nothing to do with my baby or with me. I heard it said that he had raped me and that he had seduced me with sweets. My mother should take him before the law. We answered neither yea nor nay. My interest now was in finding a way to support myself and my child for my mother agreed that I should have nothing more to do with Manichsingh.

My mother had begun part time higglering but had to leave off to deal with her pregnancy, her baby having a willing, capable and socially acceptable father and she therefore did not need to rush off to help herself. Not so her 16-year-old daughter. I took over her practice. I could use her boxes to take my wares to the market; I could get her space on the truck and in the market when I got there.

Whether buying from the farmers, selling in the market or travelling to the market, you found many men who were willing to take on a 16-year-old and her yellowish brown baby. The offers were many. The one I took was from a young farmer. He had never had a live-in woman and I had never been a live-in woman. We did well for about five years during which time I made him a father for the first time and the second time. We were quite a family. He treated my Indian son as well as he treated the other children. I was a good businesswoman and had no objections to helping in the field. He had two sisters who were higglers like me. My success bothered them and they claimed that the land my babies' father was working and from which he was sending me with the products to market, belonged to them for it was family land. This was very unfair for even if it was family land, it was his energy that was making things grow on it. I wouldn't quarrel with them; didn't want to create dissension in their family, so decided to leave. My babies' father was vexed with me: he knew that there were very many men out there who were interested in me. And I knew it too. In fact, by the time I had made up my mind to leave, there was someone willing to accept me and my children. This new man, my husband now, worked in a big butchery in Kingston and got a weekly salary. The baby father that I was leaving behaved so badly that I was glad to leave him. He took every opportunity to tell the whole world that my new man worked at killing cows as if this was a shame, and he swallowed cow's balls raw. He would ask anyone willing to hear him out, how could I leave him for a man who sucked cow's balls. I was ashamed of him.

I am now a married woman with six children by three fathers. My husband is a real husband and father to all six children. I chose well. But not even he could stop me from having to band my belly bottom time and time again, as I had done while I was carrying him, over the behaviour of Mr Manichsingh's son. He steals. My neighbour is building a house and as soon as lumber is dropped at her house, it appears under my house. I have to ask her to send for it. He loves electronic appliances and especially cell phones. And steals them. As soon as somebody misses one, he or she appears at my house to collect it and the appliance is very often there. It is as if nobody expects any better of him for no one bothers to press charges. I never thought of it before, but perhaps the village loves him – he is as pretty as a film star. Perhaps the village is sorry for him given his beginnings. I don't know but the boy has raped. Why does a pretty boy like that have to take by force? I think he is just bad, made so by the way in which he was made.

Women sometimes have to leave their children on their own for a weekend while they are at the market. My son took to visiting one of these homes. I think the girls really thought he came to protect them but instead he overpowered one and raped her. That is her story and I believe her. He is lucky. Rape is seen around here, if the rapist is a young man and pretty like my son, as the girl's fault although this one was only thirteen. The justice of the peace who heard this case, must have felt like the rest of the village that the girls by letting him in the house "asked for it" for a pretty boy like my son, could get any girl he wanted. But this crufty girl with no grandmother, no roots in the village...she must have asked for it. He was let off with only having to show himself to the police, once a week and keeping out of trouble for three months. I think about that girl and wonder if I was raped. The girl had to be taken to the doctor. I didn't have to. I was not forced. My son is worse than his father. I suppose this is my punishment.

My Indian son has vanished. I worry. There is so much gruesome killing these days. I fear that he could be beheaded some place or his body chopped into small pieces by some opposing gang. I don't know if he is in a gang but I don't put it past him. Someone saw him far away, got his phone number and address and I have been trying since then, to get in touch with him to no avail. My boss tells me to stop worrying about him: If he wanted to be found he would answer or turn up; that perhaps I should respect his need to be alone at this time; that he will come back to me when he feels he can. I am going to take her advice. I will leave him and stop worrying.

My other boys are in the army and in the police service. They are all older than the girls. I like that for I feel that they can keep the girls in order both by being older than them and by the fact that they are in the armed services. Perhaps that is what I lacked growing up and what made me cooperate with Mr Manichsingh. I was the first child and as such had nobody to draw my ears, to watch my movements closely, though perhaps those who could, my mother, her lovers and my aunts, saw no need of this, me being such a good girl and devoted to my lessons. A bigger brother I think now, might have guarded me against Mr

Manichsingh's shows or hit me in the head when he heard that I went into the school toilet with Ivan. You can see that I am just fishing. I still have no idea why I let Mr Manicksingh into my privacy for I could have pushed him out of the toilet and told him that what I did with myself was my business. I knew that he dared not report me to my mother for she would have just chased him away and insulted him.

All my sisters and brothers have done well. I was worried that I might have set a bad example for them. Perhaps what I did was so outrageous no one would be foolish enough to do likewise. They are in teaching and nursing and no one has had a baby without marriage. I don't know if my daughters know the story of how their eldest brother was made. How would it help them to know? Perhaps they could learn that sex is not a game, that there are social pre-conditions to having the male and female sex organs meet. I guess that is it. And that it is not good enough to know what you should do or shouldn't do. It is more than knowledge; it is action or non-action as the case may be. Manichsingh vanished about two years after his son was born. God is good. I didn't have to see him and be reminded of his nastiness and my what? Stupidity?

This was not a mind that she liked to run upon her for it was a flat bed truck of eight or sixteen wheels slowly, slowly and deliberately going over her little puppy dog self, doing her worse than it had Uncle Jasper. She had experienced it time and time again and was left feeling not only pulped but extremely tired. Like a Sisyphus, and wondering as he must have done concerning his heart and liver, why did they keep growing back, why not extinction and the end of the flatbed truck running over her or him carrying that stone up the hill?

Aunt Jennie whose mind seemed to have nothing to do but run on her or have her in it locked in like air in a tyre, would soon be coming with her flat bed self to tell her as she always did, that she wasn't looking after Carlton well; if a man is not happy at home, of course he will wander and even beat you and she was lucky he hadn't beaten her yet.

Aunt Jennie was *her* aunt, not Carlton's; he was only her nephew-in-law, so how come she was always diving in and taking up for him, not even asked by him? Aunt Jennie having run her mind on her, would bustle in with great delight and view her remains, she felt, a dirty foot cloth on which scores of feet had wiped themselves in the muddy October rain, and she'd pile her wheels on again, back and forth. The bustling in was not a twenty-four hour thing. Aunt Jennie was no doctor; she was a nurse, in for the long haul. Her business was to get her niece to do better.

When the children came Aunt Jennie found a lot wrong that she had to stick around to fix – they had liver spots and that would take a week of baths in quaco bush. Or breaking out was found in one head and if it was in one, it would soon be in all three scalps and she would have to tread the long road to go to Mass Simeon's doctor-shop to buy whatever Aunt Jennie prescribed, for the pharmacy around the corner did not carry the stuff Aunt Jennie wanted, and feeling that the things she was asked to buy leaned more on balm yard than orthodox medicine, she couldn't send any of her helpers or even have her husband drive her there, and have them feel that her aunt was dealing in darkness.

The worse of it was that Carlton did not like her being around and expected his wife to stop her from coming. He could not perform in his bedroom with that snooping witch around. No wonder Aunt Jennie could pull her aside and say that she heard nothing going on 'in there', never interrupted a loving glance between 'you two'; something was terribly wrong with the marriage and it was always the woman's fault. Coming back home to her with the children was totally out, so Ursie had better do something about it before the crack turned into a split. Her response was to hold her head down and occasionally shake it from side to side. She felt like the willy penny she had saved in an empty shoe polish pan when she was four. The tin was marked one-O-one and she had taken to shaking it ever so often to assure herself that her first money was still there. Perhaps her shaking of her head was really to find out if her brain was still there or if Aunt Flatbed Jennie had really crushed it into non-existence.

Her helpers must have been wondering the same thing for she had overheard Winnie and Pauline saying that she was shaking like the girl they called 'Shakehead Babe'. She knew 'Shakehead Babe' and she knew that there was some sympathy and respect for the shaking of Babe. According to the story she was known to be able to swim like a fish and curse like a sailor. What Babe had told the man, was a saying about the place. "Him see har clothes one side and see har a swim and him tek off fi him and come eena the water, waan put question to her just because she kinda funny with her head just a shake-shake so. Wan tek advantage of the poor girl. And is not her fault why she stays so. When she a baby her little brother love her so much, him lift her up — couldn't manage har and she drop from him pon her head and it start shake from that. Babe tell the man a word, all now it a hat him."

That was Babe. What story did she Ursie have for her head shaking? And was love anywhere a part of it? Nothing that should not make her eternally grateful for all that had happened in her life, she mused. No fall or hitting of the head. Aunt Jennie had 'taken' her. As she told it, "She fell in love with Ursie, those big bright eyes and that engine hair like my mother's and took her from the impossible marriage that her mother, her baby sister June, had made and left for her children on her death. The man so careless, the government had to step in and take the three boys to Alpha Boys' home. The girl was not even his daughter, and thirteen years old, can you imagine how he would have used that child if I hadn't stepped in. Still hoping he didn't get to her before I took her away." That was her story. Was there love? Perhaps she had had too much of it. Babe's brother loved her. Did she love him? She wasn't sure that she loved Aunt Jennie, though she really ought to, shouldn't she? Certainly there was no one she could tell words that would 'hat' them. So no relief could come to her from that quarter.

Ursie's problem was compounded by the fact that she did not know what signs her Aunt Jennie was hoping to see. It couldn't be lying on the sofa and doing what white people did in movies and which ought to be kept in the bedroom. Why did we have movies rated 'PG' if real people were to lay about in the open involved in baby production actions? Aunt Jennie grew her and for two years of that growing Uncle Jasper was there in the house. She couldn't recall any lying on the couch business taking place and there was no shortage of couches in the house. In fact she had never even seen Aunt Jennie and Uncle Jasper sitting on the couch and watching television together. They had never even held hands and gone into their bedroom together. In fact Uncle Jasper had done more talking to her than to Aunt Jennie. Something was strange here. Light on this question came in an unexpected way.

Aunt Jennie for all her many years of marriage had made no children. Her only sibling, Ursie's mother had died and so of course had their parents. Aunt Jennie had nobody else. Even Carlton could respect that and prepare himself to let her in when there was this odd and searing pain at the bottom of her belly. Ursie brought her home and sent for the doctor who when he came, called her to Aunt Jennie's room to ask her help with the examination. "I need to do a vaginal examination and your aunt will not open her legs. Perhaps you can coax her." She had tried. Her aunt had protested that there were several ways of doing an internal examination apart from going through her private parts. No argument could get her to open her legs. She had turned her head to the corner and muttered "Nastiness.

If I didn't let my wedded husband, Jasper do that, how am I going to let some doctor from where I do not know, do this to me." Ursie thought she heard what amounted to "Only Jasper could do that" and tried to comfort her, "Aunt Jennie, is many years since Uncle Jasper left you know. He wouldn't have been unhappy if you had taken another man. Much less a doctor's examination. He is not eager for you to come to him, you know. And if the doctor can't examine you, it could be the end for you." The doctor whose ears were perhaps more attuned than Ursie's chimed in, "Mrs Gentles, I know that you are a Christian woman and have kept yourself pure and I respect you for that. We are trained to enter you without disturbing your innocence, you are right. The only problem is that I don't have these instruments with me that would allow me to do it that way. The commonest way is how I tried to do it: most women your age, don't mind. That's why I suggested that. Pardon me."

More mumbling from Aunt Jennie in reply and, "I am not most women" could be clearly heard.

"To do it your way, I would have to take you to the hospital which seems an expensive alternative when we are not quite sure that what is wrong with you requires hospitalization," the doctor continued.

Ursie agreed to pay. After all, whatever little money Aunt Jennie had was coming to her. She could afford this extravagance; she expected that enough would be left over for her funeral. So Aunt Jennie went off to the hospital, was duly anaesthetised and examined. It was a clean steel instrument that entered her.

Carlton's laughter could be heard all around the town. "Curiosity," he said between bouts of laughter, "the old lady wanted to enjoy this thing through you. She wanted us to be making love all round the house so that she could enjoy herself vicariously."

"When since you turn psychiatrist?" Ursie asked playfully, but he turned serious.

"This was a wicked situation though, for I nearly send you to psychiatrist for this head shaking and holding down your head, when is your aunt who really need to go to the psychiatrist. Eight thousand dollars a time I nearly had to pay to get you to stop shaking your head when is just your crazy aunt messing with your nerves. Poor Uncle Jasper, he must have been glad to have that flat bed truck run over him to his death." He tickled her and asked, "So we going put on a show for your aunt when she come back?"

Aunt Jennie had sent for Carlton after her operation. He actually got her to talk about it. In fact she wanted to talk about it and took the opportunity of Carlton visiting her outside of visiting hours and therefore having her alone, to speak. She had sent for him and he had chosen this time because he had assumed that she wanted a private talk. He had thought it was a matter of business that she wanted help with straightening out as a lot of people wanted to do on their death bed. But this was not so. Carlton was to be the psychiatrist he didn't know he could be. Aunt Jennie's story was that no one had told her about 'those things' and she was quite shocked by the sight of her husband's nakedness and had asked him to spare her. She had been spared. Carlton wanted to know how Uncle Jasper managed for all those years. Aunt Jennie told him that Uncle Jasper had had his woman from even before their marriage. He had married her instead of the woman because she was a 'good girl' and he wanted a good girl for his wife and she had been a good wife. All he did was go back to his woman when he needed those things. *She* clearly did not mind those things and was apparently willing to welcome him back. She had to say for them, she revealed, that they were very respectful of her.

The woman, Dulcie, never tried to fight her or to come between them in any way. They lived close enough and had to see each other from time to time. They would bow to acknowledge each other's presence. What she further confessed to Carlton was that she couldn't understand why the man who was so considerate on his honeymoon and the years after, should in his death be bothering her and trying to open her legs at nights. This was part of why she was so glad to come to their house and she didn't want to die without thanking Carlton for putting up with her, so he was to consider what she had just told him, as thanks.

Ursie teasingly wanted Carlton to know that she didn't like how interested he was in Uncle Jasper's situation and she wanted him to know that he had no reason to seek a helper as Uncle Jasper had. With this, she took the argument into philosophical waters: "Uncle Jasper could a try harder though."

"You would a have to find a way to make it the man's fault eh, with your woman's lib," he countered.

"Unfair," she shouted and said more quietly, "Look here Carlton. What me did know when me come to you? You see Aunt Jennie and you must know that nobody didn't tell me anything either. But what you did do? Say is alright and go to other woman? You never do that. You coax me until everything was alright. Uncle Jasper coulda do that."

Carlton smiled. He had got a big up out of the argument. He didn't have to win it. But she wanted to learn more and pushed him into their bedroom and closed the door against the children's inquisitiveness.

"Carlton what is this about Uncle Jasper trying to have sex with her? Mi see the black and blue marks at the top of her legs you know. It look like somebody was hitting her there for true? How that can be? Mi ask the doctor and him say is vitamin c shortage but that don't sound sensible. You think somebody was coming through her window and trying to rape her. Though Aunt Jennie love lock up lock up so much not even air can come into that house and into her room, I don't see how man can come in and go out."

"You say it yourself," was his not so helpful answer. "Is something psychological I think. Just like how that crazy lady was teasing you into lovemaking in the public so she could see – you realize that her telling you that she didn't hear anything going on between us and so on, was to get you to prove her wrong and have us licking out on the couch or some other public place. The old lady did not want to die without seeing these things. I think the business about Uncle Jasper raping her is just a step further. She doesn't want to die without experiencing sex. And so strong is her need that she create this whole situation."

"But the black and blue, Carlton. I see that. Is not my imagination nor hers."

"Then Ursie, you don't think that if she so crazy as to want to see you having sex and to have sex, she couldn't be crazy enough to hit herself. Might even be beating up herself in guilt over giving up her real and rightful sexual activity for a flight of fancy."

"But, Ursie" said Carlton, "You don't notice sey the door lock and the pickney dem quiet and the helper dem know what them to do, them don't need you. What to stop we?" Nothing stopped them.

After an unusually long time, Ursie straightened her clothes, helped him to zip up his pants and looking up into his face, asked him, "Carlton, if you dead before me, you going come back and make love to me?" He laughed but she persisted, "Is a serious question, Carlton."

He said, "You have not been Aunt Jennie. By the time I dead, you would have given me enough to keep me going in heaven or in hell or wherever." He thought that he had given a pleasing answer but noticed that Ursie wasn't looking all that pleased.

"What happen now?" he asked.

"Then what about me?" Ursie asked. "If you dead before me what I going to do?"

"You want me to come back?" Carlton asked.

"Mi not too sure that mi don't want that, you know," Ursie answered.

"You know mi Ursie. As long as you want that mi want it too. And we always know when we ready for each other. So no need to worry. But if you want that, make sure you nor nobody don't put no corn grain in my coffin and tie me down. And don't make dem make you wear any red panty. Dem tings keep away duppy."

"But what if I die before you?" Ursie persisted in this duppy talk.

"To tell you the truth, Ursie. Me woulda go get one real woman. Mi promise sey it won't happen in this bed. It can't, because mi know sey you would come thump thump up the woman an drag me off of her, but she must have her own place and mi will tell her to burn candle fi keep you off."

"Well let me tell you something, my dear Man," Ursie said as she unzipped his pants, "You a go drink egg nog and strong back and mandingo and sarsaparilla, for from right now, you going to do all the work you can in this world, so that when mi dead, you so tired that you can't go to nobody else."

"That is ok by me," he said as he turned her around and pulled her zipper. Then Carlton had to have his joke: "Look at all of this and Aunt Jennie in the hospital and can't hear us. Promise me that as soon as she come home, we going to do a double barrel like this for her." Urise gave him a fake box. He added, "We must also thank Aunt Jennie, for she probably wanted to see that you weren't doing like her and forsaking your husband. She wanted you to have a real life."

Ursie didn't feel no way to ask her helper to go to Coronation market and bring back strong back, sarsaperilla, chainey root, irish moss and "to make sure that the irish moss sell with linseed." The helper had to have her joke too, "Like you stop shake your head now Mam."

Perhaps because she was living in the same house with her or because she had her own nurse to help her through her hysterectomy, Aunt Jennie's mind did not run on her at all in her post hospital stay in Ursie's house. Or it could be that with a better understanding of Aunt Jennie's problems and knowing that nothing was really wrong with her Ursie, her aunt's mind, when it ran on her was now more like a bicycle than a flat bed truck.

Vadney

"I did hate to pay over the twenty thousand dollars but once dem tell me is government get it and not that piece of nothing, I didn't too much mind and I concentrated instead on the bandage across his head. I was hoping that the buck and the cracked skull I give him would leave such a mark that he never would be able to forget why I do it. The man mess up my sister. He was after me first but when I see him buzzing round Evadne, I drop him and curse him out. Wanted to bring trouble between me and my sister. Don't care who dem hurt. So some of them stay."

"My sister was the brightest girl for her year at Shortwood. She graduate and come back home to teach and we were so proud of her. Not a soul try to obeah her for the whole of Nelson street think is their child and was pleased with her success. He come back from farm work with his boom box, his accent, his tapes and his lies about being in march on Washington with Martin Luther King and Million Man March with Farrakhan, mixing up the dates as only an ignorant liar can. Don't know how him never march down King Street with Marcus Garvey. Mussi never see that one on television. My little sister was full of black passion but had no true black knowledge and she draw near to this three card man as if he was the black nationalist he said he was. Then she got pregnant and of course she had to marry to secure her job. He gave no trouble about marrying because he think he was marrying a monthly salary."

"But he got a shock for she wouldn't turn over her salary cheque to him and that is when the beating start so much so that she lose the baby, telling me that is not beat he beat her. Is fight and that she give as good as she get. Liar. My sister couldn't fight fly. All this time the man putting question to me talking about how he marry the wrong sister; that is Vadney make him bad for she won't stand up to him and he know sey if it was me, me woulda straighten him out and wouldn't take no foolishness from him and he would be a much better person fi dat. Straighten him out yes! I woulda make him look like a common 'I'. That's what him gwine look like now with that mark on his head. The balding head gwine look in truth like a dot on top of that long body like how the cut mi cut him kind of separate the head into two, one part on top of the other."

The lady was talking at me. Like a mason slapping concrete on a wall, the information came. She didn't know me from Adam nor I her. I was standing in her street for the first time in my life. I had driven from my St Mary more than a hundred miles away from her Savanna-la-mar, Westmoreland; was early for my appointment and was standing waiting for 10 a.m. I was to interview some officer or other about a social development project, so it suited me to hang about outside and let the vibrations of the people for whom this project was being undertaken, get into my consciousness. What was happening here was almost too much.

The lady delivering the sense of the town to my head was very dark and squat, a well rounded 'a' rather like that which a kindergarten teacher puts on the board for her newest students – an 'o' with a stick on to it. She wore the full higgler's uniform – full length bib in heavy green, the kind that is a dress except that the back is empty, only a waist band shows there, fastened with a big button. She wore the bandana on her head. Another trowel of concrete came my way, dashed on me without warning.

"Look pon her." I had to look hard to find the 'her' that I should look 'pon'. She was hard to find though she was there, a kind of ignis fatuous, a letter which a child had pressed hard to make and had chosen later to erase. She was but an outline, a shadow. I had barely given this word thought before the echo came: "Shadow? Not even a shadow of her real self. This ya woman used to dress up eena her high heeled shoes and gone teach at school. You wan see her with her piece of stick a keep time while twenty-four or more students singing before her. The way she teach them to sing 'Roll Jordan Roll', you coulda hear the very river roll. And when dem sing 'Hush somebody's calling my name', chills run down your back. That was the choir but she coulda sing solo by herself too. Every church concert wanted her and no muss, for them make so much money from the whole heap of encore that she get. Look pon her now. If you sey 'boo' it look like she woulda run. De man beat him down so much, him don't even know who him is. Lose the job and the salary. De man vex and how come she lose the job? The lose she go lose the baby which the man lick her and cause, her whole woman system go bad and too often she bleed so much she can't even go to no work. Hear the nothing now: If we no see how him los' off the marriage for no baby, not even a salary and what him fi do with a woman whose woman system permanently out of order? Him wouldn't even send her go get hysterectomy, though doctor sey is that she need."

The ancient mariner eased up a little and I looked at the wronged lady. Truly that erased letter looked like she would run, bolt at any second. She was not as dark skinned as her sister. Hers was a washed out black and she was as flat bellied as a white mannequin. The long dress she wore clearly belonged to another time as the waist and the bodice swung around her and the flowers on the fabric were barely discernible. What could have flattened out this woman so? Her gynaecological problems no doubt left her anaemic but there was more to it than that.

I might have been meditating on this my question and not paying enough attention to the sister's dramatic presentation for she came over, actually touched me and sought to re-direct my attention: "Listen Sister" – I was now a sister too – "mi see her hand eena plaster polish and mi ask her 'what happen' and she tell mi say, she fall down and break her han. Then mi see de man and me say to him sey, 'Poor Vadney slip and fall down and break her hand. Him used to suffer with bilious and ah no one time him fall down.' So mi tell the man that and ask him if him tink that thing come back pon him. The man turn to mi an say ah him box him and him fall down and break the hand. Him never mean fi him fi fall down and break him han. Him sorry. A dat time mi jump up and buck him like how you see dem boy a buck football. De man drop and hurt the head worserer. It crack and water a run out of it. Him see taxi a pass and him stop it and go fi police and dem take him to hospital and come fi me fi arrest me. Mi have good friend and mi is a good behaving person, so mi never have to spend no time at jail."

"Now mi ask you Mam," the ancient mariner continued, addressing this captive wedding guest, "What dat fi a tell lie bout? Wha dat fi a hide?" I looked at Vadney. I was so sorry for her, a bird with a broken wing, not being able to fly away and forced to wait for the cat or dog to finish it off. What could she say? She had opted to protect the man's reputation from her blustering sister and what had happened? He had betrayed her and here she was being unmasked by her sister with all the people on the busy piazza hearing how come she was wearing this thick white armour on her hand. Here she was, back to six years old, as her big sister yanked the good arm with "come here to me" and continued her soliloquy "Don't even have hand to pull up her zip and the man lef her to come out a street looking like a hang pon nail. What is a zip that him can't pull it up. Set of wutlissness dem. Can pull down zip but dem think it hard fi pull it up."

'Hang pon nail', an apt description I was thinking: she did look like a garment hanging from a nail on a wall. 'Hang pon nail'. My people certainly had the gift of describing. The 'hang pon nail' Vadney opened her eyes, and her lips and with her zipper now closed and the dress fitting a bit better, delivered aloud: "Twenty thousand dollars! Ah gwine pay you back." Her sister didn't let this pass "Pay me back Vadney?" Then she turned to her audience for she now had more than this one captive wedding guest, "Oonoo see how mi sister get fool-fool. De man not even giving her enough money to buy food fi eat. Oonoo no see how she look like any of them half-starved dog out thereso (of which there were many) Ah wha she ah go tek pay mi back? Who ah go offer her a job with dat deh sickness wey she have?" Vadney hung her head again in humiliation. Her sister was not finished, "Mi glad you hand broke for you woulda use it change him bandage them and give him tablet fi relieve him pain. Mi glad. Mek him stay deh. Mi no mine the money. Him fi feel pain. When mi jump up and buck him, mi buck him fi you, fi Mama and Papa who mi glad gone before them see what you come down to; mi buck him fi wi grandparents, two side of them; mi buck him fi wi aunt and uncle dem; mi buck him fi wi bredda dem; mi buck him fi wi niece and nephew dem; mi even buck him fi de baby that you los' who would be my niece or nephew."

I was their sister too though God had given my parents only one girl child. God had put me on that piazza more than a hundred miles away from my home for a reason.

> Massa God ah God
> Massa God ah God
> God in the evening
> God in the morning
> Massa God ah God

I had no one to butt Harry. My brothers wouldn't. We were not higglers: this was not our style. At my wedding my father had told me that every house has a back door. I suppose that he meant that I could walk out of the situation if it was too much for me, and knowing my father that is about all he had to say. But it took strength to walk out. A man of few words and little action, my father had said his say and done his act; he was not likely to pull Harry's ears metaphorically or otherwise. He had forecast what after six years was just revealed to me. My mother said he had seen in the man I was about to marry, a naamz, his word for one who didn't know protocol, had no manners. You didn't just send a girl to tell her parents that she was going to marry you, my mother said he had said. You went to her parents and told them about yourself and asked for their permission and blessing. Today after the sermon on the piazza, I determined that I was leaving and without Harry's head damaged or my hand broken. I would find the way available to my caste: I would open the back door and walk. I had no intentions of being an erased letter like Vadney.

Harry had been so sweet. I was painfully shy. I remember sitting in a small social group with the handsome bachelor that everyone was talking about. And he was handsome. My friend was giving me first option, so I was invited to this very small gathering. At one stage in the proceedings Handsome Bachelor looked in my face, held my eyes and asked not for a date but for my name. When I replied, he said that he knew it. He just wanted to know if I could speak. I knew that I was thus struck off his list of possibilities. I say this to say how socially uneasy I was when I met Harry. It was he who brought me out and 'Baby look at me now!' as the Virginia Slims advertisement would say. I had a thriving social policy consultancy, thus my trip to Westmoreland. I was undertaking some work which the minister needed to complete his submission to the Cabinet. I often addressed one minister or the other and had even been invited to present my findings to a Cabinet sub-committee which the big man, the PM himself chaired.

Harry was still the struggling lecturer I had first met and who had told me that I was sensible and needn't worry about nonsense coming out of my mouth; it simply couldn't for there was no nonsense in my head. That did marvels for me. He had stood behind me resolutely, said when I was about to graduate that he had a holiday job for me. That was so helpful for you know that with the best degree in the world, prospective employers are still asking you for job experience. Two goods, for of course I was being paid and needed the money to outfit myself for a permanent job. We had worked closely on his project and he had listened to my suggestions and implemented some, to my unending joy. At the end of the project and after the final grades were posted, Harry said he had fallen in love with me, didn't know what to do after three years of seeing me at least once a week and would it be alright to marry. I married him – I was at the marrying age and all my friends were doing it – and he continued to nurture my mind and build my confidence until I am where I am now.

He complains now that if he hadn't been spending so much time on me and my career, he wouldn't still be a struggling lecturer; he would have at least done enough work to get appointed to a chair somewhere. That might well be so but that was his choice. I had not even set my cap for Harry. I still don't know how one would do that. I hadn't wanted anything more than a job in the civil service or in teaching. It is Harry who had put me on this path. It was Harry's choices all the way, and he had chosen to push me rather than push himself. I refused to take any blame for I know I would have been as happy teaching third form or docketing a file as I was briefing the minister. His response was to criticize me and my work most destructively. Harry even told me that it was he who introduced me to deodorant and perfume, and that if I hadn't met him, I would still be wearing all that coarse thick hair like a Pentecostal sister, pulled back and under a hat.

Vadney had sensitized me to marital abuse and I could see now that there was something called verbal abuse. That is what I was getting from my husband. But I still figured that was not as bad as physical abuse. That would have me out of the marriage in a tick. He would give compliments with holes in them. "You are a good writer. I give you that. You have to be, to get those politicos – though the very fact that they are politicos means that they have no sense – to accept this argument. Anyone with a grain of sense could look behind your findings and see that your conclusions are not borne out by your data."

This man who knew that he needed to publish now or perish, was spending time on my work! He had a computer on his desk in his office at the university. There was one at home. I used this. I would see him studiously at our home computer and know that he was into my files. I had an image of me getting a laptop and locking it to my wrist as I had seen secret service men do in films. Harry would chop my hand off to get to my files, I was sure. I suppose he wanted us to discuss work as we used to when I was his assistant for that short while before we got married. But I wasn't his assistant and some of the issues I was dealing with, I only knew because of secret files I was given to allow me to do the job my clients wanted me to do. In any case, my work was not like university work. I did not have a year in which to do anything. Every project had to be finished yesterday. We lived out of Town. While Harry's work allowed him to go into Town and the university three times a week, I had to go in nearly every day and travel sometimes as far as Westmoreland. I didn't have time for discussing academic theories and didn't think I should share my clients' secret information with anyone even my husband. That seemed unprofessional to me.

I tried to tell him this. That was when the grumbling

started. He seemed to be muttering something like, "What I made I can unmake."

I stopped at the big patty place in Clarendon Park on my way home to buy my favorite conch soup, and Harry's mumbled words kept coming back to me. Close to that jumped up in my mind a recent occurrence and I felt that the two were related because of their proximity in my mind and that the connection needed to be explored. The minister had called me to an unscheduled meeting. He had something to show me. It was a copy of a letter to the press that had been copied to him. We didn't take the *Jamaica Observer* so I wouldn't have seen it. The minister had recently spoken highly of a project for which I had done the initial research and had even called my name. The letter talked about the minister's gullibility and suggested that instead of praising the consultant he should be firing him or her. Without checking with me, the office had sent my paper to a foreign consultant and he had no great problem with my methodology nor with my findings, and did say like Harry, that my communication skills were excellent. The letter was signed by Robert Parks, the name of the great African American urban sociologist. That was a Harry touch. Was the letter writer Harry? Was this how Harry was going to unmake what he had made, unmake me? The minister said he thought I should know that somebody out there does not like me. I realized that had the foreign consultant not been positive, I would not even have heard that there was someone out there that didn't like me. I would have been blackballed as a consultant, I would stop getting jobs and nobody would tell me why and put me on my guard. I would be going mad wondering what had suddenly happened why all my clients had forsaken me.

Driving into the parking lot at the patty place, I had moved to the point where I was comparing myself to Vadney, that erased letter. She had got physical blows; I had got none. If that had come, I would have been long gone. As I sat with my conch soup, I said to myself. What Harry had done, if he had done it, was a high tech box, as bad as a body blow. If a physical blow was what I was waiting for to leave, I had had it. I hadn't like Vadney fallen. In fact I had moved up in the minister's estimation with his enforced referral of my work to a foreigner and the consequent response.

As I washed my hands in the bathroom and saw my beautiful face in the mirror, I remembered our private life. He had taken to attacking my womanhood. Shades of Vadney. He had had to be going out into the streets for some love and was sleeping with the prostitutes that he was interviewing for this definitive work that had been 'in process' on his curriculum vitae for at least five years. If I had been woman enough he wouldn't have to risk AIDS, but I had been so much in my head that I had forgotten that I had sex organs. When I countered that as far as I knew, it was the man that approached the woman and taught her what he needed and how to recognize it, and that he knew the state in which I came to him, his response was a gesture of pushing me aside, though he didn't actually touch me and with that, "Go read some decent books and find out what you lack. You have proven to be such an ungrateful bitch that I fear that if I teach you anything else in that department you are bound to go off with this skill too to your airheaded politician friends." What was he doing with me when I was not as attractive as–(call any name) and he did call names, whom he could get by just beckoning. He even cursed my hair oil. "Stop putting all this oil in your hair. Don't you know that you share a bed? You probably don't know. You never get in here until early in the morning when I am sleeping. I don't want to go to my work smelling of your cheap pomade." These comments hurt but the worst was the body blow.

I was lucky. That had been deflected by the foreign consultant. What else would he try? I would have to read the newspaper carefully. Harry's next attack would be through the press as well. That was his weapon of choice and that was what had messed him up, not little me, I surmised. Five years ago Harry had been in his ackee. Every two bit organization needed him to give a lecture, sit on a panel or give his views on matters as far ranging as global warming and the politics of Honduras. He had jumped at all of these invitations though they had nothing to do with his field of research. He even had a spot in the *Gleaner,* 'Harry thinks'. Bennet in Psychology had arrived two years later to be crowned the new oracle by the press and the service clubs. Harry's star started fading. 'Harry thinks' went to some obscure page and then vanished. Bennet went through the same metamorphosis. Environmental Studies and Russell were new. He was fast becoming the new oracle. Before Harry it had been Cumberbatch in Mass Communications.

Surely Harry could see that the press played games with them. His light will never shine again. When somebody new comes it won't be Russell's voice on Direct on CTM piped into people's houses at the choice time – relaxation after the family dinner; it will be that of the new man. That is how it goes. So Harry had better study his prostitutes and write his paper and have it published rather than wait for the public relations department of any of those media houses or any of those service clubs to call him. Nobody should have to tell him this. I wished there was someone who could tell him, for it certainly could not be me, the bitch who had robbed him of his creativity and his popularity.

As I slowed down at the Vineyard toll gate I felt a little bit of pity for Miss Mc, his mother. She had hauled him up by herself and those newspaper columns with Harry's face and those sound bites and the glimpse of his face on television were her payday. Pity started seeping away when I remembered Miss Mc's way of dealing with our conflict. We still went over to her on quite a number of Sundays. Miss Mc could not help but see that things were bad between us, for her son always found the place furthest from me to sit and I was firmly elided from his speech and even references. Miss Mc's approach to what she could not help but see, were statements like: "Shirley you don't bake again? Long time you don't bring any nice thing for me." Then I would explain that one salary couldn't cut it – nothing about my need for self-fulfilment, Miss Mc wouldn't understand that – and I had to be up and running as well, so there was now little time for baking. I suspected that this interjection was intended to bring matters out into the open but Miss Mc's tack failed miserably. All her son would do was to murmur one of his insults such as "What I make, I can unmake"or "No time for woman things."

It was not long after I had this talk with myself on the way from Westmoreland that we visited Miss Mc in our separate cars and she asked one of her foolish questions which she probably thought was a subtle probe. Miss Mc looked at my flat stomach, the result of hours of exercise and said sadly, "So Shirley, how much years now and nothing baking in that oven!" I was so fed up with the word plays and the subtle unsubtle questions and Miss Mc not seeing that her son needed help which I was not in position to give him since he hated me so, that I went down to Miss Mc's level. "No fire Miss Mc, no flour and no rolling pin. Nothing can't make, Miss Mc, and worse of all this oven not getting any wood Miss Mc." A great shame came over me and I realized that in staying in such a relationship I was no better than Vadney who at least could tell herself that she loved the man. Love, if it ever was, had flown out of the door a long time ago. I saw that I was moving not so much into the faded letter but into a letter erased with one of those cheap erasers which left black and sometimes green smears on the page. I should have driven from Westmoreland straight to the divorce lawyer in Kingston. To make up for that lost time, when I went, I would also check the real estate man and see if I could find a little apartment somewhere in Kingston, nearer to my clients. I am doing this, I told myself, remembering the sister's poem –

> When mi jump up and buck him
> Mi buck him fi you
> Fi Mama and Papa
> Mi buck him fi wi grandparents on two sides
> Mi buck him fi wi bredda dem
> Mi buck him fi wi uncle and aunt
> Fi wi niece and nephew and
> Even fi de baby that you los' and that
> Would have been mi niece or nephew,

for many other people. I would be taking action for Evadney who penniless and still in love, cannot leave her tormentor.

Valerie

I met her at intake. Her normal skin colour is black but she was hyper black as if she had been rolled in tar. Her hair still showed signs of chemical straightening but it hadn't been combed for what looked like weeks, so the straightened ends stood erect. Dress: she had on a black under thing like a slip. The straps were broader than the normal slip so it could have been a light black dress or a tunic. On top of this she wore a green tunic several sizes above hers. It could not be hooked as the zipper had been taken out. She and her green tunic made you think of Jesus's pierced side. Perhaps this was a school uniform too short or too tight and flung out of a house as useless. In my mind I applauded this strange-looking young person for having the faith or determination to walk off the street to which she clearly belonged, up the stairs to an office which must look to her official and intimidating. She was very clear about what she wanted and asked for this even before she accepted the seat I offered. She wanted me to find her baby. She didn't want him back for he was comfortable with his father in America. She just wanted to borrow him so she could show Harold that she could have baby. I got her to go back to the beginning.

"Well how it go you see Mam, is after I age up in elementary school, that all this business start. They say I pass Grade Nine Achievement Test and I must go to high school but I could only go for one year for my grandmother couldn't afford it. She say is better I look a work. So she buy powder and lotion and deodorant and mi fix up fi go look work. Not far from us they have a big settlement with pretty concrete house so we say someone there must want a young girl to tidy up and things like that. I walk and I walk and I walk and nobody didn't want anybody. Then I go to a upstairs building. Is not like this. It have four different parts and I knock on the first door and a man come out and say to come in. I go in and see him fixing breakfast. He have two egg in a pan with oil upon the stove and he tell me to sit around the table and I see him break one more egg. When this one egg cook, he put it on a plate on toast bread and pass it to me, then he put the other two on two slice of toast bread for himself and sit down. We eat and I tell him I looking work. He look me up and down and say you look nice and you smell nice. See the bedroom there go and fix up the bed. Then he come in the room and put his hand round mi waist and lift me up and put me in the bed and pull his belt and drop his pants and come in the bed with me. He wasn't rough like the first man who did that to me; but he did look a bit vex when he say, "So you do this already." He give me five hundred dollars in one bill and say mi can come back to breakfast any Monday morning that I feel like."

"Mam, I walk and I walk, I walk through the whole place and I don't get no job but I glad I have the five hundred dollar note to give my granny who I not even so sure is my granny for she never able to tell me anything about my mother or my father but she treat me good. I tell her everything and she say 'That no bad. You get one day's work.' Every Monday mi go to him and is the same thing happen except for one time I go there and I was seeing my health and he say not to come at those times there."

"Is like the man know everything about me Mam for one Monday about a month from that time when I was seeing my health, I go and he say he wasn't expecting me for don't I seeing my 'ladies'. I know what he was talking bout and I tell him No, I was not seeing it yet. So we do what we have to do. I continue coming and now he start ask me if mi see mi health yet. And I answer No. He want to know if I vomiting or anything and if I feel funny. And is true. I did feel like my stomach upset and like I bilious and I tell him and the man start to cry say: Look what him do, and him never mean no harm. Him apologise to me say is just some company him did want, for him wife and children gone abroad. Him cry living eye water, you know Mam. Then him start worry bout him wife, what him going do, for his wife, if she ever know, will take back the visa. Is that time that I know sey the man married and expect to go to America."

"Then mi really start show and mi granny follow me and come to him and him give money to me for clothes and tell my granny that he will play his part. Apart from the clothes money, he give Granny four of the five hundred dollar bills. When we leave the house, Granny sey, 'Him want wi fi dash wey the belly. That is what him give these four five hundred dollar bill for, but we nah do that for this baby can go to foreign.' Mi stop go and is only Granny go to him now on Mondays. All this time he still sending money. When the baby was about a year old, Granny sey 'You start go back on Monday and take the baby with you for what him giving now is for you and me. When him see the baby him will give the baby him own money'."

"The man so glad to see us! He lift up the baby and start

to play with him and sey how this is his first and only son and him glad to have him. Him start crush up food from his plate for the baby. Is yam he eating with his egg this time. Mi know sey people like that feed dem baby with special feeding, so mi tell him that the baby don't use to food like that, to give me money to buy baby food for the baby. Mi will go up a supermarket go buy it. Mi tell him sey him can play with the baby while mi gone. The supermarket far and while mi a walk, mi ah sey to myself: The man like the baby and the baby like the man. Him never even cry when mi leaving him. Why mi shoulda go back fi him? Why mi no just lef him wid the father?"

"With that mi take the bus and go right back to Granny and tell her sey the man have the baby. She ah quiz me and mi tell her lie sey the man sey fi leave the baby with him. The man never really sey that but my granny glad now for she sey the baby gwine go with the man to foreign and once you have a chile in foreign, you can go there yourself and then you can file for other members of your family. All now we don't even know the man last name and not even sure sey the first name he give Granny is real but mi start tek out mi passport. Then Granny start to ask mi how mi gwine live without the money from the man, for mi did give up the Monday thing. When mi no have no answer, she sey she know somebody who want a girl and she send me to Harold."

"Harold did have him own mechanic shop and thing front of where him live so him wasn't poor but him did look dirty when him come in and mi didn't like this for my baby father never look like that nor smell like that. Moreover Harold did have greasy clothes that him want me to wash and mi couldn't manage it. When him see say mi caan manage, him go on so bad, mi tell Granny and she get one kerosene pan at market and she build fire eena her yard and boil the oil out of the clothes before we wash them. When him smell the clean clothes, Harold love me up, like my baby father. But my Granny landlord now start complain sey is board house him have and the fire in the yard too dangerous. Moreover those clothes don't belong to anybody in the yard, so is business my granny and me running and Granny gwine have to pay extra for water rate. With that now, Granny sey mi deh pon mi own."

"Now mi nuh know how fi mek wood fire. Moreover mi no see no wood fi go mek the fire so even though Granny sey mi can borrow the kerosene pan, what bout wood and ketch fire? So Harold clothes no wash good. Mi see electric iron and ironing board and mi sey to myself sey perhaps if mi put seam into the pants, Harold wouldn't mind if the black and the oil still een to it. So mi start iron the one that mi wash in my own way. The iron melt the oil in the pants and give off a bad smell and stain the iron and the iron board. When Harold come een and smell the smell him vex and when he see the iron and the iron board, him seh how is not even fi him own. It belongs to the girl who he was with before me and how she a go gwaan bad when she see her iron and her iron board in that state."

"Then him take to cussing me sey how mi can't do anything, mi can't even breed. Two years now mi mongst him and mi don't breed. Mi face him up and tell him sey mi can breed for mi have pickney and mi tell him bout the baby and the baby father and seh the baby is in America with the father. Is that time him cuss mi worse, tell mi how mi fool; if the baby did have passport; how him fi travel if him no have no passport. So mi say to myself, mi a go look fi mi baby and get passport fi him, but when me go there, mi neither see man nor baby. Mi tell Harold, him sey the man mussi gi way the baby and gaan to him wife a foreign. Mi look, mi ask question, mi go a police station – no man, no baby and Harold still a cuss mi. But mi know my baby gaan a foreign for the father did smooth and brown and him mus know somebody can let through the baby widouten any passport, so mi never worry bout the baby. Just the cussing."

"One man come deh come gi out him car, good good car, Mercedes Benz and him spy me round the back a siddung with mi hand a hold up mi face and him sey to me sey 'A lovely girl like you shouldn't be looking so sad and poor.' And him give me a card with an address and sey they need young girls there. Mam, mi never know sey a slack house, you know Mam. Me so glad fi dis place for dem give me mi own room and the lady come een an look and see sey mi no have much clothes and she carry mi go to store an suit me out. All carry mi go to hairdresser and get mi hair cream. But come the Friday night, Mam, man knock pon mi door, come and pounce mi up. No matter you lock the door, you know Mam, for every room have an extra key and them give the man that at the desk, so all him have to do is put the key in the lock, push out your key if it is in, turn the key and come in and do what him like with you. Dem don't even talk to you, you know Mam. Just arms you up. An is not one man for the night. After him done with you, another one come in and so on until mi run wey."

"Mi go back a Harold and him call me mule and run me. Mi go to mi granny but she get a boyfriend and him sey him can't take on nothing more and she sey she old and can't afford to lose him for him is her bread and butter, so mi have to go. Mi box bout and box bout; sleep pon newspaper pon side walk; eat wha scrapses people throw wey and wear wey dem no want but mi don't like the life and mi tink sey if Harold know sey mi ah no mule him we tek mi back and mek mi try fi have a pickney for him, for mi check round and check round and know sey him no get no other women yet. Not even the girl whe leave the iron and the iron board don't come back."

What could I do for this dirty bundle called Valerie save hug her and tell her to forget the baby. I didn't think it was gone to America but even if it was in Jamaica it would be under a name unrecognizable to her and either in a government institution, in foster care or at best adopted. I advised her to forget trying to prove herself to Harold and further advised her that if she knew how to wash and cook and keep house, Harold would take her back and if not Harold, somebody else. So she should try to learn how to do these things well and I knew of a place where she could go and learn to do these things.

I know that part of her dirtiness was deliberate. It was contrived to keep men off so I was hesitant about my next offer. "I can send you somewhere to get cleaned up and pass some exams if you can, you know."

"But money and job," she said, "You can't out there without money or job, you know Mam, for without them you can't flash off the man dem and me nuh wan go back into any of them house there Mam for the things the man dem want you to do is not natural, and you have to do it, for them say them buy you. And sometimes when you deh pon the street, dem don't even buy you. Dem kidnap you and carry you weh and do dis and dat to you, dem and dem friend, you know Mam, and carry you back tear up tear up and withouten a penny. Happen to pretty girls. Thank God mi no pretty."

I persisted and said, "We can get you cleaned up and send you to school to learn whatever you think will get you job and money, but whether you learn and get a certificate is up to you and with a certificate is how you get a decent job that can keep you from having to deal with the men." She looked skeptical but I guess she was tired of being dirty and agreed to go with me.

One beautiful black-skinned girl! With the muck washed off and the straightened ends clipped from her hair, Valerie looked like an Ebony model. She did get some subjects – office management and data processing and English A. I was at her graduation. I assume that the school got her some kind of job. I lost sight of her for years but met her again recently because of our church's outreach programme. Our church group ministers to the fallen on Hanover Street, a street of body selling shops. I was disappointed to meet Valerie in one of the houses on one of our crusades. Let me give her this: she was one of the organizers of the unit that invited us. She must have seen my disgust for she asked me if she could have a few words with me after the session. I could not but agree. She started off by saying that she knew how I felt but that she was not sharing her body for money. "I am with the administrative staff. I am using the skill I got through you to make my living." I answered that the distinction was difficult to see and she had a whole essay in response.

The people who came there knew the difference and nobody had ever asked her to do anything but balance the books, and no client had ever done anything to her except hand her money through the bar of the cashier's cage. She let me know that this was not so in the job to which she had gone after training. "I am telling you this because of who you are, Miss, but please consider it a confidence as I have assured Mr… that he was forgiven and it would go no further." Mr… had expected from her more than he knew she had been trained for. It was a constant physical fight, she said. She felt that he had scant respect for her "no" because she was coming from the reclamation centre. The other employer was no better. This current one, at her interview had made it clear that consorting with the clients was out, nor was she to expect any special attention from him. "He couldn't know," she said, how much that meant to her.

"I am not that attractive, Miss, nor is 'for sale' stamped anywhere on me, yet most males of the employing class see me as that. All the other girls who graduated with me and were put in employment say the same thing. Some gave in and are now driving new cars given them as pay for those kind of services and have townhouses; those of us who refused still have low paying jobs. The girls who work not in the office but in the homes of these rich people, have a similar story. Some even had the wives come on to them. And some even worse than that: The couple want you to be a sexual tool to both of them at the same time. Your church has to have a mission, she said, to the upper class to teach them respect for their own and other people's sexuality. "I minister to these girls, Miss. That's why you are here," she advised me. "Don't look askance at them or at me. We make an honest living doing what we do without tricking anybody. Miss I would like you and your group to help with the schooling of the babies who are born to girls here."

I felt ashamed and determined to learn some more

about sexuality and its expression in my social class. I felt ashamed because I was foolish enough to believe that Mr… and the others like him whom we had so closely vetted, could be what we didn't know they were. And their wives, those saintly sacrificing creatures could be lesbians on the prowl! What else could we do? I suppose we have to accept this child's statement and now warn the girls we send out that these powerful people to whom we send them could be sexual predators. Then I asked her about her private life and dreams for I really did want to know.

"You won't believe this Miss," she said "but Harold turned up here. I couldn't talk very much with him for I am not allowed to fraternize with the clients. But I did manage to find out that he has not found himself a woman yet and has not got the children he wants. I learnt too that there is a place with him for me should I need it."

"Then you will now leave this place and go to him?" my romantic view of life led me to ask.

"Miss" she replied, "I have a good relationship with the girls and have learnt that Harold is a regular. It is not a nice thing to say but we are not sophisticated enough here to deal with contraception before or with abortion after. Girls do get pregnant. Harold has impregnated no one. Perhaps it is he who can't have children. I want love. You get this from the child you make and the person who helped you to make it. I couldn't tie myself down – and tying down is in it for me – to someone who can't give me children, so Miss, I am still looking. To tell you the truth Miss, if my baby father should turn up married or unmarried, it would be difficult for me to run him or for him to escape me. He was a nice man, Miss especially when I compare him with my two employers and the man who came before him. He could cry, Miss, and he knew when something was out of order even if he was doing it."

I hugged her. I couldn't bother to let her know about and accept that the great man had the freedom to say to his wife, "I can't come to you in the States. I have new responsibilities here." He had never once, if the story she gave me is true, sought out her grandmother to find where and under what physical conditions she and his child were living before she brought the child to him. I would bet her that the episode with her was not meaningful enough for him to mention it to his wife. Let somebody else pull that comforter out of her hands. Also I could state with a measure of certainty that the man had given away their baby. The one thing of consequence that Valerie knew about the man, was where he had lived.

The records which I researched established that a man with that address had taken a young male child to the police station saying that it had been abandoned to him by a young woman who begged for money, asked him to keep the child while she went to get food and never came back. The police had even remarked to him that the baby looked like him but they had taken the child and placed him in government care. The social workers had jumped on the case – we prefer to have children joined to their natural parents rather than in government care – hoping that the man could lead them to the mother. He had flown the coop. Clearly the reunion of Valerie with her baby and its father was out.

I hoped that she would find a way of seeing this bastard for what he was and would soon find a fertile man who liked her and whom she liked and preferably single. Meanwhile I would think about what she had asked: a way of helping the babies born of the commercial connections. I was hoping too that we could work on getting some of her sisters into training for some jobs more appropriate than the ones they were now in.

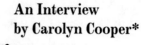

**An Interview
by Carolyn Cooper***

INTERVIEW–April 2, 2012

CC: In July 1951, you had two short stories published in the *Jamaica Times* when you were a mere child of ten. Why has it taken you so long to come back to the short story? This is your first collection that is being published.

EB: I really can't imagine why; except to say that I like the longer form of fiction. Reading it, I'm not a short story reader. I like to read the novel and I suppose I like to write the novel. So these short stories, I'm not sure where they came from at all because it's not my form. But here they are.

CC: Apart from the form though, the themes seem very familiar. For me reading these stories, it reminded me so much that border crossing is one of the issues that you've been writing about in all of your novels and in your academic work as a historical sociologist and you seem to have characters in this collection who are crossing borders of class, of colour. Tell us a little about what motivated you to write to start with, before we come back to these stories.

EB: What motivated me to write and to write fiction is that I'm coming out of Sociology which I went into because I wanted to be of assistance to my people.

CC: And who are your people?

EB: My people are the African Jamaican people. The people who are the descendants of Africans enslaved in the New World. Those of us who are very rarely portrayed in books or in films and therefore don't really know very much about ourselves because we haven't been doing the research on ourselves nor have we been talking about ourselves. And I figured that the fiction – I tried the other thing – the fiction is easier to understand ourselves through, thus my interest in the fiction. As a matter of fact, I really came to fiction in a very odd way. I was doing a study, a Sociological study, and I was so fed up with the quantities – five per cent of this and ten per cent of that – that I took to writing on the questionnaires. I took to doing pen pictures of the people that I interviewed. One of them escaped merely because one puts up questionnaires and on the back of this questionnaire was this short story. I entered the short story in the Festival[1] and it got placed. So I figured, now here is another way of getting my people to know about themselves. The short story. That was how me and fiction came up at all.

CC: That's amazing. So this was when?

EB: Some time in 1972.

CC: So between '51 and '72, those two decades you were doing your "conventional academic work"?

EB: I was mostly doing my conventional academic work.

CC: And here now the short story just shows up on the back of a questionnaire. That is a wonderful post-modernist kind of moment. So let's talk about it some more. Fiction as an alternative discourse to dry academic questionnaires. But in a sense the questionnaires were trying to get at, as you say, African–Jamaican history and culture.

EB: Yes, just about anything about us.

CC: Do you remember what was the short story you wrote on the back of the questionnaire?

EB: The story that I wrote on the back of the questionnaire is the only one that happens to be in this collection.

CC: Which one was that?

EB: I'm not quite sure what it's called.

CC: Do you remember the name of the character or the situation?

EB: The situation is Zackey and Rosa. Yes Rosa.

CC: Tell me what you remember of the experience writing it then and now in this new context of a collection of short stories. I'm intrigued by this idea that you're doing this fool fool questionnaire and thinking, "let me deal with this matter from another perspective".

EB: Well it would have been how this woman Rosa comes to be Zackey's 'wife'. How does she do it? She gets a dream. His grandfather, whom he had cared, dreamt her and said Zackey need help, you go and take care of him. You're not going to get that in a questionnaire. A sociological and anthropological questionnaire is not going to deal with that.

CC: A sort of celestial online dating!

[laughter]

EB: Yes, yes, yes. Heaven came into it. And then of course, there is the other thing that she herself, now, when she dies, she dreams him and tells him whom he must choose as her successor. So it's really dream dating.

CC: That is such a wonderful idea, that the dead should be able to control the life of the living. A lot of young people, students, maybe high school students will read this collection, hopefully in school and some of them may not know even this notion of dreaming because unfortunately our educational system tends to marginalise 'folk discourses' so a lot of this stuff is you know, not in the consciousness.

EB: I even just hate the word 'folk'.

CC: Everyday people.

EB: Yes, everyday people and their world views.

CC: So let's talk about the dreaming-people business.

EB: Ok, well, if you're in connection with your people and if you understand that when you put someone in a coffin and put them in the ground, that is not the end of it. If you understand that, then you're kind of open to them coming back and helping you. As a matter of fact, when you're ready to pray, if you're praying, you might pray to the standard God, or Jesus or whatever, but a number of people expect to hear something on this issue that is breaking your heart, from your people who have gone on before. And a number of people get messages and operate on what they have been told by their people who probably understand the situation better than Jesus. If I can say that without being hit down by [...]

CC: Yes, or seen as blasphemous.

EB: They understand it better. They probably passed through

it. Or they saw you growing up so they understand what your soft points are, what your weaknesses are and so they can tell you fairly easily where you ought to move.

CC: Or who is a good man for you. Much better than the conventional wisdom.

EB: Or a good woman for you.

CC: Well the other world has always been a part of your fiction. I think of *Myal* for example. You want to talk a little bit about *Myal*? About how that whole sense of the spiritual meeting with the so-called natural. The supernatural. How does that figure in your world view? To use a fancy term.

EB: In my own world view there is a book which is supposed to be out very very soon, that I did the foreword for; and in it I tell the story of my first close-up relationship with the other world. I was sitting in sixth class. No it wasn't sixth class, it was fourth class the first of the middle division classes.

CC: So about how old would you have been then?

EB: I was about six...when I heard somebody scream. And the class looked at me. I didn't know who screamed, and they didn't know but they were looking at me. It wasn't odd because I was bright so they would look at me if there was a question to be answered. So I just let that pass but I realised at some stage that it was I who screamed and the reason I had screamed was because some people were taking me away and I didn't want to go with them so I screamed and the point at which I screamed they let me go.

CC: Wow! Ok. It is a pity during the slave trade we couldn't just scream and get let go. So what else happened after that, in that moment?

EB: Nothing else happened but I just know that I was being taken away by some people who I didn't want to go with. I suppose if I had gone with them I would have sat down there and I would have lost my brain, lost my head or something like that. I would have been a shadow because they would have taken my essence away. So I'm very aware that these things can happen, and that these things do happen.

CC: And you deal with that notion of transmigration of souls in *Louisiana*.

EB: Yes I do. I deal with it all the time and you see bits of that kind of thing in *Myal*. I operate on that level in my personal life as well as in my intellectual life. I'd very much like to pursue all of this some more. As a matter of fact, as you know or probably do not know, I had fellowship in psychiatry for a year in a medical school at the University of Washington. I came out of that wanting to go to Africa to study African psychiatry. It didn't [materialise] for some odd reason. Odd reason being that the letter really inviting me to come, crossed with another letter and didn't reach me in time. So I couldn't accept. That is one of the things, you just know that that should not be because that wouldn't have happened if it was to be.

CC: Well in fact in *Jane and Louisa*, your very first novel which didn't start life as a novel as we now know, you do have a character Nelly who is on a fellowship in the States in psychiatry and she's meeting black Americans. Was that bit in the novel based on your actual...sort of semi-autobiographical?

EB: It would probably have been though I can't remember right now. I know that *Louisiana* is much more in this area of psychic, psychiatry or anthropological psychiatry than any other of the works. But you don't find this in any other story than in 'Rosa'. And in Rosa's case a lot of the stories here, there are things I knew about in my youth that I just wanted to find answers to and couldn't find any answers so I had to make up the answers. For instance in Rosa's case here now, I know about a woman who went to Linstead to the hospital, wanted to come home to die. They didn't take her home. They took her home in what they thought was a dead state and when she was going up the hill – they were taking her up the hill – she just started speaking. Well she didn't speak for long. They took her and in a couple [of] days she had really died. But she insisted, her spirit was so strong that she came back and died in her house.

CC: That's a powerful story.

EB: Yea, well nobody is going to take a story like that from me, because I know it happened. So all those that say these things don't happen, I *know* that it happens. That there is this other world that I operate in as well.

CC: Well remember Mortimer Planno died twice, you know? You remember? The Rasta elder he died and then came back and really died a few days later. So it does happen. So tell me about some of the other stories in the collection. As I said, I see the border crossing, the class, the uptown and downtown getting together as one of the issues. But tell me, as you were writing the stories, what you felt were some of the overall concerns that you were trying to bring out in these stories.

EB: Well the main concern was as I said, I had unfinished business. Things I knew about but didn't know the end of so I really had to make up the end of them.

CC: What were some of the unfinished stories.

EB: Take 'Pauline'. I know a case which I've been watching for some time. And I just didn't know how it would end. Well there it is 'Pauline' ends with the girl getting out of the Orthodox church and running away from the Orthodox. She doesn't cross borders. She makes up her own little society. And then in a sense she's willing to cross the border on her own terms. So I knew of this girl and I watched her struggle. We never talked but I just watched her struggle and I figured that I needed to put it down. And not only put it down, I needed to put it down for Pauline who never asked me to put it down. But I needed to put it down because, these stories here, I feel that they are people who have these stories who need to see these stories and need to have other people read these stories.

CC: Yes, these twelve stories are all about women and their relationships and I was intrigued by the title that you gave the collection, *The World is a High Hill* which actually comes in one of the stories. Tell me about that idea about the world being a 'high hill.'

EB: Well to tell the truth *The World is a High Hill* is not my creation. I asked a friend of mine, Angela Heron, to read these stories and it had a very ordinary title such as "Stories of Jamaican Women" and she said "No, no, no, no, no, that can't happen. This book ought to be…" and she gave the name.

CC: But wasn't that name in the story?

EB: It's in the story, yes. I think it is 'Cynthia'. This is the girl who got herself involved emotionally with a white man; and I know people like that. I can think of one young woman when I was on campus.[2] I always wondered how she managed with that relationship. She was just there alone, very attractive black girl but the only one who was involved with a white man on campus that we knew about and eventually there was a marriage. But I've always wondered about the interior of that relationship.

CC: So you mek it up?

EB: I mek it up.

CC: So what did you make up? How did you, from the outside, read this relationship? Since you so faas.[3]

EB: I read the relationship that they didn't even know what they were getting into. They were just friends, and they were friends because they felt the same about certain things and they just didn't even know that they were sexually attracted to each other. And never even knew that they wanted to be life partners. It never struck them, they were just enjoying life.

CC: And that idea of the world is a high hill, what do you think that image is supposed to [convey?]

EB: The bush you have to go through, you have to go through a whole heap. I've always said – I don't know if I'm right, or I don't know if I'm still right – you have societies in which the norms are very very clear. In our setting the norms are not clear and most of us have had to go through and establish them for ourselves. So the world is a high hill. You're walking through bush; there is no pathway; you see it in *Jane and Louisa* - there are no pathways that are actually clear for us to travel. We have to make up these paths and bush[4] them out as we go ahead. So it's a high hill.

CC: For me the image was more positive than this arduous journey of walking through [the] bush and cutting. When I read it I thought 'The world is a high hill' suggested all of these possibilities in life that perhaps sometimes we get stuck down on the level and we don't realise how much more there is – this high hill – that there are these heights to be attained. Maybe I'm just a product of Caribbean schooling where you keep climbing Jacob's ladder, you progress and move up.

EB: Well you know I always say that when you put something on paper and you send it out there it's no longer yours. It is for people to deal with and you accept. So I accept and I am happy with your interpretation.

CC: But I am also persuaded by yours that the high hill suggests what you have to go through to get what you want. Tell me about some of the other women in the other stories.

EB: I'm very particular about 'Lilieth'. I read 'Lilieth' to a gathering on a verandah one Sunday, mostly of men because I wanted to hear their response. 'Lilieth' always makes me feel like crying because so many of us started our love life, for want of a better word, with a married man. And I'm not knocking married men at all because some of us got [a] very positive understanding of ourselves and enjoyed the relationship. But it is painful for the people who are in it; painful for the young girl who is having her first relationship; painful for the man – and people don't think it is painful for him but I think it's painful for him; painful for his wife.

CC: Why do you think it's painful for the man? If it was so painful him no would ah leave the young girl alone and stay with his wife?

EB: But we can say the same thing about her. If it was so painful for her she would have gotten out of it a long time ago. Or painful for the wife – she could lick him down and walk out.

CC: Well maybe the wife wasn't in so much pain because she glad fi get somebody fi help her with the work.

EB: Well there's all of that but I just feel that I haven't seen it written about. And then that story begins with her not even knowing that black people had 'love life'; love affairs, because we [are] so [tuned] to looking at the movies and looking at literature [but] we don't see ourselves in it. So she had no model from there; she didn't even know what was happening to her when it was happening.

CC: So how did the men on the verandah respond to the representation of the married man's sad lover?

EB: Well one of the comments that one man made was "But all of us into that already; all of us go through that."

CC: That sounds like one of your brothers.

EB: It wasn't one of my brothers. And I know – from being fass – a bit of his story. I know that he started off a young lady, a very important young lady, on the path and I imagine that nearly everybody has gone through it, whether it be the men or the women. But I thought it was necessary, if somebody wants to cry [and] reads this, it's an opportunity, it's a therapeutic opportunity for somebody who has gone through and found her way out of this path.

CC: It's interesting that you use the metaphor of therapy for fiction and I wondered, with your background in psychiatry, if you wanted to talk a little bit about the therapeutic function of fiction not just for you as the writer but also as the reader.

EB: Yes, yes, well for me even as the reader, when I got the proofs of *Jane and Louisa* I cried; because *Jane and Lousia* was written at a time when I was going through…I was coming back to Jamaica and on a number of levels that was an extremely difficult thing. As a matter of fact I think I got physically ill; not really mentally; but physically ill. I think I got a thyroid problem out of trying to deal with living in Jamaica when I came back. I'd left the United States – it was the time of Black and the time of Woman – as a black woman and I was high up on the totem pole. I came back to the University of the West Indies in Jamaica and I couldn't be lower.

CC: What year was this?

EB: It was in 1968.

CC: But that was the time of Black power. In fact that was the year I came to UWI…so sorry I neva know you dem time!

EB: I came back two weeks before the Rodney thing.[5] And going down in the street with my hair natural, Lord, I got so much flack. Even in the market. The market women didn't like hair that was cut, it was against the Bible and your hair is your glory….Oh Lord it was a very, very trying time. And especially since I was coming back from psychiatry with the *intention* of theraputising the whole of Jamaica.

CC: And nobody was a tek you on. Dem tink seh you mad and a you doing the therapy.

EB: Yes, I was just mad. And somebody I liked very much said to me "Well if you come back wid yu head like dat you mus' expect that people going to treat you like that."

CC: Well head like dat now is working class head.

EB: I don't know, my head is still like how it was [then].

CC: But natural hair means you're a pious religious person that doesn't believe in press[6] hair; or you are radical black power.

EB: Well I don't think I was even seen as radical black power because I didn't have on sandals; I didn't have on African print. I was just dressed normally but with my head looking not so right.

CC: 'Normally' because the Jamaican 'normally' was Eurocentric dress.

EB: Yes I was in Eurocentric dress.

CC: No I'm just teasing you because you said you were dressed normally.

EB: Yes Eurocentric dress and the head is abnormal.

CC: So the hair may have been a metaphor for what was happening in your head.

EB: Well my head was quite right. I know that my head was right, right where it should be. But in terms of the cultural dress, I was culturally in a corner. I remember I was doing this work on abandonment of children and going into the social work offices – the government offices which I had to go in to collect data – and I went into one in Highgate which is my parish and the officers there just scorned me. Really scorned me. They didn't speak to me, they just scorned me and I heard them saying, "Smady fram

University can carry dem head so?" And then I knew that it was my head that was the problem. But I lived to see one of them sit before me, being interviewed to come into the social work programme, with her head like mine. Because after about two years, that head was popular and popular especially if you wanted to go to the University. But there it is, so you see it's a high hill for me.

CC: Yes absolutely. So literature as therapy for the writer, but have you seen your work being read and impacting on people?

EB: Well you know, and this is one of the reasons I'm happy this work is out, in that people have been saying I'm inaccessible, you know your students say inaccessible. I don't think anybody can call this inaccessible. It is here for them and as I said, who want to read and cry can do so. The one example I have, you know that *Jane and Louisa* was once done in a play?

CC: It was Earl Warner who adapted it?

EB: Earl Warner, yes. I was sitting in the play one night and when I came out I heard two women talking and one of them saying, "look how far Nellie gone with her life and mi no even start organise my life yet."

CC: Oh, wonderful.

EB: And I said boy, well there is one person at least, who has been able to identify with what I was trying to do because it was supposed to be therapeutic.

CC: Even though some of my lazy students initially pretend that they can't manage *Jane and Louisa*, it's for me a great victory every year I teach this course and I've been teaching it now for over a decade and a half, that you get them gradually being seduced by the book. "But Miss it not so hard" and they write essays on it, some of them write about it in their exams, so it touches them because they begin to identify with Nelly as a Jamaican woman whose story is not so unfamiliar after all. The clever way in which you approach it, the plot structure not being so coherent helps to destabilise them and then gradually when they come in and start to get the more straightforward story they can deal with it. These stories are certainly accessible but they're also very engaging. I just found myself being drawn in. The stories are really very compelling.

EB: Well it bothers me that they might just read them and then say that this is another book and fling it down. You know like you buy a truppance *Star*,[7] you read the *Star* and then fling it weh. But you cannot fling away *Jane and Louisa* nor any of the others. You have to read it several times. But I don't know that these are...

CC: But the accessibility I don't think is going to make people take them lightly. Because you don't want to believe that the thing has to be a high hill for you to understand it you know.

EB: Understand and empathise with.

CC: Well one of my favourite stories was the one about the couple from school.

EB: 'Kishwana'.

CC: Kishwana, seducing this middle class boy.

EB: She didn't seduce him!

CC: Yes she seduced him. But seducing is not necessarily sexual seduction you know. He was just engaged by her world.

EB: Yes he was engaged by her world and engaged by *her*. Her figure and her brightness.

CC: Brains can be seductive as you know.

EB: Well why don't we use the word attract?

CC: Well why not seduce?

EB: Because seduce has some negative things. He was attracted to her; and I like the fact that he was attracted to her because she was bright. A number of bright girls in school have just been in the corner and nobody picking them out.

CC: Yes but part of the problem I think is that for many black women, we have not been projected. How we look is not recognised even now in the media – as sexy – unless it's really downmarket sexiness as what you would see in certain settings when they're advertising certain kinds of alcoholic products. That is when they use the 'healthy body' female. And when they're advertising the upscale products they use the slim 'brownings.'[8]

EB: Well I would like them to start projecting that bright is sexy. So that young girls can see that 'mi bright, mi pass, mi get mi ten CXC[9] and mi get mi four CAPE[10] subjects. Mi bright! *And* dat means seh mi sexy. Man out dere want mi.'

CC: But the problem is that you have to help the young men now to see that bright is sexy because a lot of them are not seeing bright as sexy. So that is why this little yout' has to be bigged up.

EB: Yes, yes, we big him up.

CC: And remember his parents tried their best to manipulate for the girl to go overseas thinking that that would mash up the relationship.

EB: Well I'm not quite sure about the mother. He wasn't quite sure about her; whether she wanted to separate them or whether she was just a real woman champion who wanted to see this girl succeed.

CC: Which is your favourite story, if you have one? Or maybe that's not a fair question to ask.

EB: I'm not sure that I have one because they all touch different parts of me. But I suppose the one that engages me most is the one about Valerie. 'Valerie' always makes me want to cry.

CC: Talk a bit about 'Valerie'.

EB: Valerie is this girl who pass(ed) her Grade 9 and couldn't go further than one year at school. And then she went to look work and there was no work except for this man who was making his breakfast and who give her a work – if she want to work she can come every Monday. And out of that came a baby which she assumed would be going to America with the man; although it didn't have a passport but because the man brown and smooth-skinned and *must* know somebody who can make the baby go through without any passport. Brown and smooth-skinned was so important to her that she believed he could cross any border.

CC: And that he would want the baby.

EB: Well she thought that he would want the baby because he

was playing with the baby and saying it was his one male child. I feel sorry for the Valeries. And when she says that she has to sleep on newspaper on the pavement and how the men come and don't even pay you sometimes, they just kidnap you and carry you away and tear you up and fling you back on the pavement. But it doesn't happen to her because it only happens to pretty girls and she's not pretty.

CC: So then your ugliness is a protection.

EB: Her nasty look too was a protection; because if you're looking too bad they're not going to come and steal you away. So of course we all know that there are some people who have to make their living in this way. But there she is. And I could see this place nearby Portmore where they have these houses.

CC: Portmore back road?

EB: Back Road. I've never been to Back Road but I've heard of Back Road and I think of all these girls who we can't find. Every night you see them, these 16-year-olds that can't be found. And I made the connection. I needed to understand that and I think I kind of understand it better with 'Valerie'. With writing 'Valerie', I came to understand the Back Road existence, and how these girls got there and what is the life for them.

CC: You mentioned the fact that *Jane and Louisa* was turned into a play. Have you ever thought of writing drama?

EB: Well I have. The Emancipation Ritual at Woodside which we do every year is a kind of play.

CC: Well I think of that more as a Ritual as you say; but I was thinking on a less grand scale.

EB: I read 'Valerie' in Toronto and people were asking the same thing; saying this thing ought to be dramatised. I'm not quite sure I see how it could be dramatised, but as somebody there said, so much of what is happening is happening in her head how do you dramatise that? But I haven't reached as far as that. If somebody wanted to do it, of course I would collaborate and try to do the script but for me right now the only other place I'd like to go with this thing is into audio.

CC: Well that's interesting too, there's a lot of dialogue in the stories which would lend themselves to adaptation.

EB: So you didn't find Arthur foolish, in 'Kishwana' which you said you liked?

CC: No, foolish? Why?

EB: In the things he didn't know about living in the innercity; five people living to a room and so on.

CC: No. Young people are insulated from that kind of reality. You take how *you* grow up as normal. I loved them trying to work it out, how they going to stay on the bed on the floor. It reminded me of that song Marley wrote which says, "I'll share the shelter of my single bed...This is love that I'm feeling." You get that sense of youthful love that really lasts.

EB: Yes, because I myself in the early days of doing anthropology have gone to places and wondered about the sleeping arrangements. How do people manage to stay in this one room; sleeping and bathing, because the bathing used to bother me. How do these people manage to look so clean, smell so good in places where I know there's no running water and where they're six people together in this hot room? How they come out looking so good?

CC: And the whole notion of privacy now is changed because if you're accustomed to having your room by yourself and you have that private space as opposed to people who have to be sharing, that kind of intimacy, you wonder what it does to the relationships, positive and negative.

EB: I remember working in an agency with two white women from Canada and one of them dated Black men. And she was telling me that her friends asked her all the time, "How do you kiss him? Can you see him?" And she tried to explain to them that you don't need to see somebody, you sense a person. That came back to me too in dealing with Arthur; that some people have to learn to sense things. Some people are brought up understanding that you sense things.

CC: But those foolish people who thought the Black man was invisible because he was dark. It's just ridiculous.

EB: Well her friends did ask her.

CC: They must have been jealous.

EB: They might have been but they just didn't understand it.

CC: The logistics of it.

EB: Yes and Arthur just didn't understand how you stepped down without stepping on somebody in a room that is full of bodies.

CC: So you sensing it is carrying us back to where we started with the extra sensory perception of the spirits coming back to manifest themselves in the body. The distinctions between body and spirit.

EB: Yes and your being in a natural state of sensing. You sense the people coming from way over; you can sense a thief; you should even be able to sense somebody who is going to rape you; you should be able to sense all of those; step out of the way of a gun. I'm sure people who live with these things more often than we do understand how to body shift.

CC: Tell me about one of the other stories that you find particularly engaging coming out of a particular experience. Because it sounds as though all of these stories come out of actual experiences.

EB: Ok! Well let me talk about 'Lily'! I wrote 'Lily' because I think that we suffered so much from Gerda that I had to write 'Lily'.

CC: Who is Gerda?

EB: Gerda is the white woman. When he [Lily's boyfriend] went over to America, Gerda came into his life and he came to tell Lily that he would like to investigate this route. So I've written 'Lily' for all of us of the late '60s who had a black boyfriend who was so full of Garvey and so full of blackness and who got you to cut off your hair which your mother spent her time trying to grow, and then come and tell you that he wants to experience this relationship with this white woman. A lot of people of my age went through that and it was painful.

CC: So Gerda became the ideal that needed to be explored.

EB: Yes, he needed to explore Gerda, and he eventually goes off with Gerda and is bold enough to say that if we think we suffer, people like Gerda have suffered as much as we have – the boldness to be saying things like that.

CC: But I think in general though, these stories are triumphant stories about women – women as survivors.

EB: I think so too, they went through it and got over the high hill.

CC: And it's more than just surviving. You read the stories and you feel it's a celebratory affirmation of women. I think that is something positive. Would you want to describe yourself as feminist in terms of your agenda in this collection?

EB: No, I don't want to describe myself as feminist at all. The reason that these stories are about women is because I am a woman. I know about women and I know what we have gone through and I wanted to put it out there as I said, probably for therapeutic purposes, or for the historical record that we went through some of these things. But it's not part of any feminist agenda.

CC: How do you define feminist agenda that you wouldn't see what you've done here as feminist?

EB: I see feminists as "Ray, ray ray ray! We've made it over the men" and I'm not about that.

CC: But feminism is not about making it over the men.

EB: What is it about? I really don't know then.

CC: No, I think feminism is about what you've done here. Women claiming power, and some of it is over men particularly in these stories; because a lot of these women triumph over men who really set them up as victims. But it's not only that kind of man that you find.

EB: There are men and women that set people up.

CC: But I don't think feminists are anti-men; they're really anti-patriarchy; and patriarchy is a system that does oppress men as well. So you must call yourself a feminist.

EB: I'm *not* a feminist. My ideal is man and woman getting together. This is how I see it.

CC: But feminists support that.

EB: Well is the later day feminists, not the feminists that I had to deal with initially when they started off their thing.

CC: But how do you remember those old school feminists?

EB: I remember the old school feminists as definitely anti-men; and even the black women who went into it many of them just became lesbians – wanting to have nothing to do with men at all – and a lot of them had the 'Lily' experience and so moved off into women's organizations. We're all women together, black and white women together.

CC: Well feminism means different things to different people. If you were to label yourself, and which you may not want to do but how would you label yourself?

EB: I have no problem at all. I am a descendant of Africans enslaved in the New World. That is me.

CC: But what does that really mean? Because a whole heap of people were descended from Africans enslaved in the Americas and have no particular identification with blackness.

EB: Well a lot of them don't but this is one of them who does. So you can add to that, whose life purpose is to help us towards healing and towards standing up straight and taking our place.

CC: You would definitely say that a lot of what has happened to black people in this part of the world has happened in an attempt to dehumanize. So as Rex[11] would have said 'smaddyfication'. I don't know if that was original to him.

EB: I heard a black woman in Dakar say: black women and black men were equally destroyed. We can work together to stand up.

CC: I believe that all of your work has had this positive agenda. 'Agenda' even sounds so militaristic. But the energy that is in your work – from the conventional academic, historical sociological [to the] creative writing – is really affirming the possibilities of Africans in the Americas reclaiming power.

EB: Power, yes power is the word I want to use.

CC: And agency.

EB: Yes agency and power and getting up and walking; walking strong and walking proud. And doing the things that are also… well having children and having men and so on.

CC: Well Ms Brodber, it was lovely to talk to you and I really do hope that once this collection of stories comes out, a lot of people will read it because they will get to understand what you've been doing in so many of your other books. And that it will open up to the next one, and the next one. Big respects.

EB: Well yes, I'm hoping it will do that because this is really my gift to people who say they can't read the other stuff.

CC: And high school children I think will enjoy these stories. I think it could be used as a textbook for the lower levels of the school ladder because most of your books are university level.

EB: I believe just about *anybody* will enjoy these. I'm looking forward to the publishers selling a great many of these and giving me some of the money.

CC: You deserve good royalties.

EB: Yes, good royalties should come from this.

Notes

*Carolyn Cooper is Professor of Literary and Cultural Studies at the University of the West Indies' Mona Campus where she teaches Caribbean, African and African American literature.

1. The Jamaica Independence Festival is an annual cultural festival held in Jamaica on the first Monday of August showcasing literary, fine and performing artists.

2. 'Campus' generally refers to one of the three main campuses of the University of the West Indies situate at Mona in Kingston, Cave Hill in Barbados and St Augustine in Trinidad and Tobago.

3. 'Faas' is a Jamaican colloquial term meaning inquisitive.

4. 'Bush' is used in Jamaican dialect as a verb meaning to clear land of bush and shrubbery.

5. Walter Rodney was a Guyanese lecturer in History at the University of the West Indies Mona campus and an outspoken black power activist. In October 1968 he attended a black writers' conference in Montreal, but on his return was refused re-admittance to Jamaica for 'carrying on activities which constituted a danger to the security of the nation.' This sparked a demonstration by University students which degenerated into riots in which three died.

6. 'Pressed' hair refers to naturally curly hair that has been straightened with a heated metal comb.

7. The *Star* Newspaper is a Jamaican daily tabloid newspaper.

8. 'Browning' refers to a light-skinned black woman.

9. The Caribbean Examinations Council (CXC) is the main governing body administering examinations for students at the secondary level across the Caribbean.

10. The Caribbean Advanced Proficiency (CAPE) is an academic qualification awarded in a particular subject by the Caribbean Examinations Council. It is generally taken in a number of subjects by students above the 14–16 age group in higher secondary education in the Caribbean.

11. Ralston "Rex" Nettleford was a Jamaican scholar, cultural icon and social critic. He is best known as the founder of the National Dance Theatre Company and as Vice-Chancellor of the University of the West Indies (1996-2004).

CPSIA information can be obtained at www.ICGtesting.com
Printed in the USA
LVOW040821150912

298844LV00001B/2/P